REFLECTIONS

Mark Insingel is a young Dutch writer wnose concerns are
similar to those of Beckett and the French nouveau roman.
This is a brilliant and provocative attempt at coming to
terms with reality where the factual mingles with dreams
and nightmares. A rearrangement of possibilities, actions,
encounters, conversations which make up man's existence.
The author neatly packages his highly personalized way of
looking at life in these reflections.

There is no plot in the accepted sense. An I (you/he)
figure reflects on some fragmentary experiences which
shift from reality into childhood, dreams, nightmares. In
each chapter there is an ever quickening pace towards
climax and a contrapuntal slowing down, so that the
stylistic effect is concentric. The unity of the novel is
essentially one of structure and style.

Mark Insingel was born in 1935 in Antwerp. He studied
drama and published a collection of short stories in 1966.
He has just been awarded the biennial Prijs van de Vlaamse
Gids, for his book of poetry Perpetuum Mobile. Another
volume of poetry has just been published and his new novel
appears in Belgium next year.

SIGNATURE SERIES

REFLECTIONS

a novel by

Mark Insingel

Translated from the Dutch by
Adrienne Dixon

CALDER & BOYARS · LONDON

First published in Great Britain 1971 by
Calder and Boyars Limited
18 Brewer Street London W1R 4AS

First published as <u>Spiegelingen</u> by
Meulenhoff Nederland N.V., 1968

© Meulenhoff Nederland N.V., 1968

© This translation Calder and Boyars Ltd, 1971

ISBN 0 7145 0709 1 Cloth edition
ISBN 0 7145 0710 5 Paper edition

Printed in Great Britain by
Latimer Trend & Co Ltd
Whitstable, Kent

To Hilde Sacré

'So in some way even olden things each time are first
things, no two breaths the same, all a going over and over
and all once and never more.'

'White I must say has always affected me strongly, all
white things, sheets, walls and so on, even flowers, and
then just white, the thought of white, without more.'

Samuel Beckett

above the trees sweeping steeply downwards creaking
hinges bolts chains are holding you while climbing
diagonally centrifugally the seat shifts under you above the
trees the lanterns whisk past the darkness the shouts Janna-
JannaJanna the flags flap against the poles stand in rows
flutters the red above the blue sweeps with a shriek to
above the trees beyond the red plunges down into the
depths waves Marina flits past you in a flash the flags flap
tug tug tug at the ropes on the poles in rows of on-lookers
(passers-by) follow a head pressed onto a jacket two hands
clutching the handles diagonally above the trees the searchlights follow Janna plunges shrieking with mirth into the
depths waves Marina (a handkerchief an arm a face) at the
lowest point at the point where the circle ends begins the
circle rises out of sight the face with the hands clutching the
handles continues to wave the flags flutter in the wind
around you in the delirious shouts of Janna approaches the
waving approaches the head on the jacket whirls away un-
attainably while the waving continues the diagonal turning
upwards a position in the turning is a position REVOLVING
evading till above the trees the flags come into sight the
fluttering approaching (apparently) moving the hands
clutching the handles do not touch the hinges bolts chains
do not leave the centre swivels you round itself (the mortal
danger of) feigning keeps the rotation going describing a
circular course round itself elicits the waving the
misunderstanding of rising and descending does not exist
the receding and approaching the head on the jacket (the
fear that a bolt loosens a ring breaks the fear of a
weakness an admission) sweeps in a curve into the depths
between the flags flap more fiercely fiercely Janna in the
seat shrieking with mirth in teasing (giving and taking)
descending and rising above the trees follow the search-

lights her passers-by hundreds of lanterns follow the
descending/rising while expectation becomes disillusion
becomes expectation while the fluttering continues the wind
changes direction (keeps the directions in balance) shifts the
blue to the red shifts to blue tugs tugs tugs at the rope in
vain JannaJannaJanna plunges into the depths in the blazing
light wave the flags belong to the turning belongs to the
flags (the diagonal turning to the horizontal waving) the
evading to the (illusory) approaching makes waving possible
masochism JannaJannaJanna shrieks a tormentor plunges
into the searchlights dive grazing the flags a game of the
wind called an illusion a symbol for what is invisible (not
existing) is affection for the other masochism swerves away
in the dark follow the searchlights above the trees creak
hinges bolts chains diagonally from the bar connects us with
the centre immovable in the whirling light a head pressed on
a jacket two hands clutching the handles centrifugally the
seat with JannaJannaJanna shrieks with mirth teases you
turning and slowing (slowed) down once more slowly
climbing the corners of the flags the blue flaps against the
red stands Marina (a handkerchief an arm a face) amongst
the onlookers (passers by) descends more slowly the red
before the blue descends the arm with the handkerchief
hangs down in the hundreds of lanterns the seat sways at
the lowest point at the point where the circle ends the
waving from the crowd.

The neighbours are walking in the garden, smiling. Looking
at each other. Looks of mutual understanding. Your grandfather is coming down the walk. He is wearing his tail-coat,
his bowler hat. Leans on his walking stick now and again.
Then looks, for the sake of appearances, across the water.
Frowns. Coughs. Walks on with measured steps. Mr. and
Mrs. Candlemaker are moving in your grandfather's
direction. They nod to each other, smile. Your grandfather
is level with them, pulls the corners of his mouth down,
frowns, twirls his moustaches. 'Morning, Mr. Thorn,' they
greet him. There are little lights in their eyes. 'Good
morning, good morning.' You move away from behind the
net curtains. You lean against the wall. They are walking
past the window. For one brief moment Mrs. Candlemaker
looks in your direction. She looks - for the sake of
appearances? - at the net curtains, the window frame, the
roof. As long as she keeps her eyes on the house she looks
serious. She says something to her husband. They smile.
Your grandfather turns into the little side lane. It curves
and descends steeply to the water, then rises again to
rejoin the broad walk. Here and there, in the grass on the
slope, among the nettles, the shrubs, the torn newspapers,
lies a turd. Boys and girls on their way home from school
aren't allowed to come here (sometimes a boy and a girl
lie here together, or there is a dirty man), do 'dirty things'
here, sit down to relieve themselves (two trees away from
each other), flock together at the place where the lane
touches the water. Boys try to catch frogs, whirligigs shoot
to and fro in the water, 'they're wearing their little black
coats, they are writing the great name of God.' Your
grandfather is alone, leaning on his stick, he looks up (the
walk is hidden behind shrubs and trees), looks down at the
water into which you sank Sniff, frowns, coughs, thinks of

Mr. and Mrs. Candlemaker. The water has light and dark
patches in it, it flows slowly away from the town, it
hesitates by the shrubs, the mud, the stones which children
(?) throw into it, the weeping willows hang over it like
curtains, here and there water-plants nearly reach the
surface (rise above it in places, twenty, fifty nails of a
fakir's bed), there are rusty saucepans in the water, a
little further down the handle bar of a bicycle sticks out.
The water encloses the town. Your grandfather goes right
round the walk on the inner bank. Over the bridges roads
lead to the villages (the town is a centre), the brewer's
castle is further down, by the river, horses from the
stock farm are grazing in the meadows (their number
changes from day to day), church spires rise out of rows of
houses (your grandfather knows which clocks keep the
right time and which don't). At the backs of the houses
overlooking the town walls women are opening curtains,
making beds, sewing, cleaning dishes, gossiping,
watching the passers-by (your grandfather). He combs
your hair with a parting in the middle (like a composer,
your mother doesn't like it, she's a business woman), he
puts your cap on your head, takes your hand. Mr. and
Mrs. Candlemaker smile at each other (About you? About
your grandfather?), from afar you can see them coming,
nodding to each other, smiling. Perhaps they feel
embarrassed because they've got to walk straight towards
you from such a distance, because they have to approach
you for fifty, a hundred, a hundred and fifty paces, the
walk is completely empty, birds are chirping, your grandfather and you are not saying anything to each other, the
water flows slowly between the shrubs, there is no wind,
the walk looks neat and tidy, gardeners from the council
were here yesterday with their handcarts, their rakes,
their hoes, one of them rolled a cigarette, another was
leaning on his rake, the wide strips of grass on either side
of the walk have been mown, there lies a branch, here and
there a few leaves, just as if you had put them there
unobtrusively but so that your grandfather would like it, he
understands your arrangements, Mr. and Mrs. Candlemaker
are near now, Mr. Candlemaker wears glasses, Mrs.
Candlemaker is fat, she has a red face, she has been coming
towards you for so long now, the moment is near when you

will pass each other, greet each other, she smiles at her
husband, you want to make the last few paces longer, get
the encounter over and done with, a nod is already there in
your head (Have you nodded yet? Are you nodding all the
time?), you daren't look at your grandfather, you might
stumble, it is difficult to move your feet (How do you? Do
you put one foot in front of the other? Do you stretch your
leg? Bend it?), you keep your hand in your grandfather's
hand, you are connected with each other through your
hands, you flow into each other, from his head it goes
through his arms into your arms to your head, from your
feet it travels through your hand to his legs, 'Good morning,
good morning,' your grandfather says, he twirls his
moustaches, looks from you to Mr. and Mrs. Candlemaker,
'Good morning, Mr. and Mrs. Candlemaker,' you say, you
nod respectfully, convincingly, 'Good morning...' you say,
'Good morning...', you pronounce christian names,
surnames, titles, pet names, alternatively expressing
respect, confidence, awe, sympathy, familiarity, cool
politeness, warm affection, formality, dignity, interest,
condescension, you know the correct place for everything,
you put into every greeting what is appropriate, the
neighbours nod back, the colleagues retort wittily (?),
relatives feel flattered, friends (acquaintances) play the same
game, holding your head high you walk down the road, you
have got yourself well in hand, for every weakness, for
every clumsiness you've got gestures to distract the
attention, the examining, alerted look, the suspicions...
you have constructed a vast safety system for your tight-
rope walk, no nets, no humiliations (capitulations), you
waver, the equilibrium is visibly in danger, a fall becomes
inevitable, people watch more keenly, all eyes are fixed on
you, unaware (?) that you will fall but intuitively conscious
that there's something the matter, the conversation falters,
they see you make a brusque movement, disappear. Where
are you? What's happening? You don't fall, you're not on
the tight-rope, only the music recedes for a moment,
inaudibly the needle is lowered into the next groove, 'Good
morning...' you say, 'I really mean it', 'How very nice
of you', 'Thank you very much indeed', 'After the rain
comes the sun', 'As long as there's life there's hope', 'One
can't be everywhere at once', 'I admire your attitude', you

also say (about others) 'If the cap fits, wear it', 'I hadn't
expected that of him/her/them', 'No smoke without fire',
'It's turned his/her/their head'. There you stand in the
centre of the picture, it covers the whole wall, a group of
old-fashioned gentlemen are listening, some are watching
you, one gentleman raises his hand, he addresses the others,
you are standing between him and the group, he's talking
about you (To you?), two men are writing at a desk, you
shrink back till your head is under the hand which is
pointing at you, you walk to the left, right through the
heads which remain immobile, you are moving to and fro
through their heads, past their hands which are crossed on
their bellies, they keep looking rigidly ahead, looking at
you, with cold eyes they look at a boy who is walking up
and down in front of a gigantic picture behind glass, in
which a group of old-fashioned gentlemen in ruffs and
slashed hose are listening to a gentleman who raises his hand
while two clerks are busy writing, there is no window, no
door, you look at yourself right through the gentlemen, you
sit down, get up, walk to the left, some of them have a
goatee just like your grandfather. Where is your grandfather? Which of these gentlemen is him? Is he one of
them? That's to say, in a moment the gentlemen will be
coming towards you, they will laugh, take you by the scruff,
pick you up, one gentleman edges his way through the
others, calls out something indignantly, pushes the
gentlemen aside who are standing around you making jokes,
he talks to them, he taps you on the shoulder, you walk
through their midst to the door which becomes visible while
(because) the group makes way for you, they form two rows
between which your grandfather walks outside with you. Who
are they making way for? Who is the gentleman who is
raising his arm talking about? At whom are those few grim
faces looking while you walk up and down, you show your
hands to yourself, you move close to the glass, you peer
into your eyes, at your lips which you slowly move up and
down while Sniff is barking in front of the mirror, 'Quiet',
you tell him, he takes a step backwards, looks suspiciously
at himself, comes closer again, he barks. You move
away from behind the net curtains. The lawn has been cut,
lighter patches show up. You try to follow the lines. There
are no lines, there are only transitions (they are always

transitions, people always talk of lines). In rust-coloured
and bare patches there are bristly streaks, gigantic eyebrows. The smooth, well-kept carpet is teeming with
patterns. It encloses the house. From each window, from
each room, you look down on it. The path leading to the
front door, the drive to the garage, the terrace, run
through it. The house is a centre. A town on the map, a
ship at sea. The lawn is a no-man's land, it is a construction of polite formalities, forms of convention (forms of
transition). In the house it is quiet. On the roof (In the
attic?) birds are scratching about (Mice? Rats?). The
scratching moves with you from room to room. Is it
moving? Can it be heard in every room at the same time?
You go outside, walk round the house. A blackbird (one) sits
quietly on the top of the roof. You climb into the attic.
Light between the beams. Nothing moves. You go back to
the rooms. The birds (Mice? Rats?) are scratching about.
The scratching accompanies you. You get used to it,
'Pulpit,' your friends tease you. 'Pulpit, hahaha.' You
stop passing on your grandfather's stories. Also your own
stories you keep to yourself. They're all of them too young
to understand when you talk about flowers, about Our Lord.
('God is dead', says Johnny, the freethinker's son. 'That's
not possible, you stupid,' you say (says your grandfather),
'God is eternal'. But Johnny has gone back to his game of
football, he can't keep up a conversation for two minutes.
All the boys can do with their mouths is boasting, calling
each other names, rattling off their lessons. Moreover,
Johnny has got a bad father.) 'You'll get used to it, my
boy,' says your grandfather, 'Don't take any notice of
them.' Your grandfather is a saint. He doesn't take any
notice of people. 'Only the Lord counts', he says. He walks
right beside the canopy in the procession, next to the
monstrance with the Sacred Host. He wears his best (his
blackest) tail coat, his moustaches are like two thin paint
brushes, in his white hands he holds a glowing lantern, he
nods (unperceived by the people) approvingly at you, you
are kneeling on the kerb, Mr. and Mrs. Candlemaker are
kneeling five persons further on, your grandfather is one
of the distinguished gentlemen walking beside the canopy
in the procession, Our Lord is the Lord of Lords, he is
the Lord of your grandfather. 'Pride is an art understood

by few,' says your grandfather. 'It means disengagement,
loneliness. The others are jealous, they call it arrogance.'
Are you proud? Footsteps (?) approach. The path to the
front door connects the house with the road. It is part of
the house (of the road). You lie with your ear to the
parquet floor, you hear it as if in an adjoining room. It
isn't birds, nor rats. It is short and measured, A
KNOCKING which becomes clearer, will stop, presents
you with a choice (forces a decision). In the only room
overlooking the path the blinds have been lowered, you are
left guessing. It starts again, the needle slips back into the
previous groove, the knocking starts again from the road,
it comes through the front garden, past the bathroom, past
the cloakroom, past the lobby, the knocking begins again
in the pipes underneath the house (Is it underneath the
house? Is it already underneath the house?), the pipes
gradually grow warm (the radiators grow warm), in the
cellar the central heating hums, you walk past the window,
children are playing in nearby gardens, the lawn has been
cut, a dark green carpet with bare patches, with gigantic
eyebrows, sparrows are hopping around, there are a few
leaves lying about, as if you'd strewn them there, as if you'd
been in the garden, seen the path where the knocking
continues, you live with it, you're getting used to it, if ever
anyone rings the bell (if anyone ever wants to make contact
with you/wants to intrude), you will be surprised as if you'd
never heard any knocking, as if the ring was unexpected,
fate announcing itself, death itself is there, the doorbell
may only be a sign that the knocking has ceased, it is after
all only a preparation for the ring, it is still play-time, the
girls are playing hopscotch, skipping, the boys play
football, run after you, 'pulpit', they shout, 'Pulpit,
hahaha,' they have yellow teeth, they are crowding around
you, they've got hands, knees, their trouser-pockets are
stuffed, yours are empty (otherwise it doesn't look nice,
says your mother), the girls are sorry for you. Do the
girls like you? You're shy with them, you kick your feet,
'Scoundrels', 'Thickheads', ('Philistines, schoolmasters,
money-makers, body-builders'), you cry, you sob, you
see shoes, knees, fists, there's a hammering in your head,
a thumping, a pounding, the bell goes, you shuffle in the
line, the playground is full of straight rows, the barrack

square, you march through the town in wide rows, you sit
in church, there are hundreds of rows in the market square,
the leader swings his arms, the slogans drone, the songs,
fists are raised, in the loudspeakers mother superior prays
hail-maries, you walk with your paternoster on your
stomach, mumbling, thousands of bees are buzzing, the
seargeant majors click their heels, shout, soldiers present
arms, you make an about turn, cross your arms, under the
watchful eye you walk to the classroom, no one is teasing
you now, the girls don't pity you. Where are you? Where
are Mr. and Mrs. Candlemaker? The squares, the streets
lie in the sun, thousands, millions of bricks have been
placed one beside the other, one after the other they have
been cemented down, been picked, weighed, placed in
millions of rows from which they can't be removed. Where
is your grandfather? Your mother? Your mother is too
busy in the shop, she has put you somewhere in a row, in
a nice one, a little to one side, but near the front, in a
square which she herself thinks is very nice (smart,
distinguished), a large dead square in the sun. Can she
remember where she put you? Sometimes entire squares
(nations) are broken up, taken away on lorries, replaced/
not replaced. But where is your grandfather? Are you only
you when you're with him? When the boys are teasing you?
When the girls are sorry for you? Your grandfather and
you see Mr. and Mrs. Candlemaker approaching in the
distance, on the walk, Mr. Candlemaker wears glasses,
Mrs. Candlemaker is fat, she has a red face, they smile,
if you two weren't your grandfather and you, but anyone
(boys from school/soldiers/nuns/mothers with children)
they wouldn't be smiling, so it's you two who are coming
towards them, and you two are you two, you're not the others
(you are different from the others), not your father either,
who is painting the house, he has got heavy tins of yellow,
blue, red, green, white, he mixes the colours, he stirs
for hours on end, calls your mother from the shop, asks
her 'Is it all right like this?', goes on stirring, fills the
tins, empties them, tries out some samples on the door
frames, the samples become less and less yellow, blue,
red, green, white, they become less defined, you can find
no names for them, you say 'reddish-yellow-whitish-blue-
greenish-yellow...I don't know', 'This is all right,' says

your father, the tins stand on the verandah with the labels
yellow, blue, red, green, white, with in each one the same
colour which isn't a colour because it has no name, it
doesn't exist, something only exists if it has a name, if you
can put a label on it. 'Surely you can't paint with that,
Daddy?' you say, 'with something that hasn't got a name?'
But he leaves the tins on the verandah where Sniff sleeps,
where the washing hangs, where the clogs with the
geraniums stand. 'Daddy is a clever man,' says your
mother, 'He can mix colours like no one else.' You cry all
morning, 'I want to bury him here', you say crossly. 'But
we haven't got a garden', say your mother and father,
and your grandfather isn't there. 'The dog has licked the
paint, he's been poisoned'. 'That isn't paint,' you say,
'paint has got a colour, you can call it yellow, blue, red,
green, white, but you can't call this anything, this is
poison, poison is something that hasn't got a name,' you
say to your father, 'you made it in order to kill Sniff, to
paint the whole house with, and if you aren't poison yourself
you'll die of it too.' 'The child is overwrought'. You lock the
door, get undressed, your pullover, your trousers, your
socks you put away tidily, by the time your father has run
up the stairs you're dressed, the shop bell rings. Is a
customer arriving? Or leaving? Will your mother remember
before dinner that you've been punished? She calls from
downstairs, you shout back, hurry into your trousers, pull
the door open, 'I'm coming', you put your pullover on, she's
not coming upstairs, calmly you buckle your sandals, you
whistle as you go down the stairs, you walk thoughtfully
between the rows of washing, between two sheets, from one
alley into another, between two vests of your father's,
between a night-shirt and a bath-towel you move from one
thought to another, the sun shines through the dormer
window, connecting the alleys, the shop bell tinkles, a
door slams shut, you don't touch the washing, you don't
brush past it with your skin, you don't press your head
into it, you don't stand motionlessly between two sheets
with only your feet showing underneath. Is your father
going to stay out till this evening? Has he simply put Sniff
somewhere without actually hiding him? You ought really
to be able to hover when you walk, your feet touch the
floor which touches the wall which touches the floor of

your mother and father's bedroom, your mother who is in
the shop stands on the floor which touches the walls which
touch the floor of her bedroom. What have you got to do with
her? With your father? With this house, where everything
touches everything, where nothing has anything to do with
anything, this noisy (profane) mortuary where at any
moment a door can be pushed open, your father stands
before you, your mother, they were looking for you. Were
they looking for you? Are they looking for you? Who are
they looking for? What are they looking for (do they
want)?, 'That child is always alone,' they say, 'What does
he do all the time?' they mean (Is this a question? Do
they ever ask questions, like your grandfather, who says:
Do you like this? What do you like best? - But your
grandfather isn't there), you press your ear against the
door, inaudibly you push the little bar aside, you hear your
mother busy in the shop, you skip several treads (every
tread might creak), you look in the stove, in your father's
work-shed, in the lavatory, amongst the tins, Sniff is
lying on top of the potato peels in the dustbin. Unnoticed,
you clamber over the wall, you hold the paper bag pressed
against you, you run through the gardens, past the cafe,
through the gate, you're in the street. You walk through the
town, anyone recognizing, addressing, stopping you, will
receive a kick, will be rendered harmless. The walk
looks tidy, the water flows slowly between the shrubs, the
wide strips of grass on either side have been cut, there
lie a branch, a few leaves, just as if you'd strewn them
there. But why isn't your grandfather there? Where is be?
You feel the little head, the legs, it is terrifyingly limp,
you roll it up like a sausage, it comes undone again, it
doesn't exist any longer, it has still got its name but it's
becoming colourless, it sinks away in the water, it
becomes water. Mr. and Mrs. Candlemaker are approaching in the distance, they smile, they've noticed you,
you're along with them, you can't go back, you can't hide
in the bushes, they call you, they're after you, Mr.
Candlemaker wears glasses, Mrs. Candlemaker is fat,
they'll tell on you, your mother stands at the foot of the
stairs, she's going to have a look in the attic, Mr. and
Mrs. Candlemaker are walking past, 'We saw your little
boy on the Walk', says Mr. Candlemaker, 'He behaved

very oddly', says Mrs. Candlemaker (she's sly, vicious,
slimy; people who always smile are like that), 'He's
not allowed to go there by himself, is he?' Your father
comes home, he too has heard all about it, he's going to
poison the house. Where is your grandfather? You can't go
back home, you can't go back to school, you stay with
Sniff, but Sniff is dead, and you're alive, you are you. Then
how can you stay together? You let down all the blinds,
close the curtains, turn off the heating, lock the doors of
the rooms. Through narrow slits, through slit eyes the sun
shines into the room, you can't trample them down, you
can't hide them under a coat, a blanket, the stripes cut
your bed in two, tall, thin figures stand on the walls, on the
ceiling, the knocking starts in the front garden, comes
past the bathroom, past the cloakroom, past the lobby...
starts in the front garden, comes past the bathroom, past
the cloakroom, past the lobby...starts in the front garden.

One by one you re-read the letters, you seal down the
envelopes, it isn't too late, you can throw everything into
the waste-paper basket, go and play tennis, shake hands,
make family visits, you can tear them in shreds one by one,
do puzzles, write new letters, illegible ones, forget,
ignore the addresses, you can simply be happy, have a
wife, a business, a shop, for instance a stationery shop on
a corner, looking out on the traffic, through the busy streets
you cycle to the post office, one by one you re-read the
addresses, the names are not names but expectations, fears,
premonitions, you read: Main Street, King Street, rue
Bonaparte, Inselstrasse, Owls' Drive, rue de la Commune,
you push them one by one into the slot, they fall in the
basket, this is irrevocable, you've got two days, a week at
the most, you've got to stay indoors, <u>nos actes nous suivent,</u>
you have won, lost, you are hated, loved, you live in various
places at once, a gust of wind makes the water ripple, the
paper boats wobble, they float to the centre of the tub, they
drift apart, 'Hold one in your hand,' your auntie Milly
crouches by you with her camera, you hold one paper boat
by its mast, you watch the bird, two boats capsize, your
grandfather teaches you how to fold them, you keep on
folding more, paper is there to be folded, to be let down in
the water, you look so sweet in your sailor's suit, you hold
the boat between your fingers, the wind knocks the others
down, they get stuck together, you laugh, you've got such
round cheeks (What have your round cheeks got to do with
the water? With the wind? With the sinking ships?), you
ride on your grandfather's knees, your eyes sparkle, you
tear up a thousand boats into shreds, you shriek with mirth
while your auntie Milly looks through the little window, she
presses the shutter, the postman is at the door, you sign,
write down the date, people know where you live, some

have your photograph (Who? Anyone you're unaware of?),
your curriculum vitae (Which one? Who has which one?),
'No, I didn't know,' people say, 'I hadn't expected that, are
you sure of it?', 'Did he tell you himself?' Will the letters
be torn up? Put away? Which ones will be torn up? Which
ones put away? You greet, you say 'Good morning-good
afternoon-good morning', 'How do you do', 'Thank you very
much indeed', 'Good morning-good afternoon-good morning',
they say, 'What can I do for you?' 'I quite agree', 'The
pleasure is mine', you wear your blue tie, cuffs, Main
Street, you think, rue Bonaparte, Owls' Drive. Don't they
receive your letters? Don't they arrive? Do they get
interchanged? You become entangled in (strangled by) a
net of data, of contradictions, they surround you with
smiles, their courtesies drive you into a corner, they're
standing around the garden, on all sides, 'Good morning,'
'You've got a lovely garden,' 'I send letters,' you call out,
'I - send - lett - ers', you sob in your pillow, your father
comes into the room, pulls the sheet off, your nightshirt is
rucked up, he pulls it down roughly, drags you out of bed,
it <u>must</u> not be rucked up, it must always come down to your
feet, you must pray, ask forgiveness, feel cold, do
penance, your father talks cheerfully, laughs loudly, you
hear your mother laughing too, you tuck up your nightshirt
very high, march through the room, press your body against
the mirror, their bed creaks, your father talks in a low
voice, in front of your grandmother's photograph, in front
of the class and the teacher, of your Reverend Uncle Henry,
you raise your nightshirt right up to your armpits, point
with your willy at your Reverend Uncle, at the class, you
dash back into your bed, pull the sheet over your head,
wait, holding your breath, your father prays out loud, your
mother responds, she murmurs, you can't hear what she
says, your father leads, again and again, he accuses her,
convinces, commands, your mother responds impersonally,
only so that your father can lead again, to make it possible
for him to confess his faith, to give his confession
meaning, to carry his banner, his candles, the crucifix
hangs over the door, the statue of the Virgin Mary stands
on the mantlepiece, your grandfather and your grandmother
are witnesses to what your father says, to what he does in
bed, your Reverend Uncle Henry too, your aunts, your

uncles are all stuck together in the photograph frame above
the dressing table, you cautiously creep out of bed, you
turn the door-handle, peer through their keyhole, your
father is moving about wildly under the bedclothes. Does
your mother know that you're standing there? Does she feel
your grandfather watching, your grandmother, your
Reverend Uncle, the uncles? She just stands there smiling
while your father shows everyone to their places, the
uncles stand in front of the ferns, the aunts sit in front of
the uncles, you lie on the bearskin with Sniff, your father
cracks jokes and everyone laughs, (everyone laughs and
your father cracks jokes), he quickly jumps amongst the
aunts, he stands in their midst in the photograph, you lie
in the centre of the photograph at his feet (you have to
mortify the flesh), you play in the garden with Sniff, 'That
child is alone too much,' 'I'd almost say he's withdrawn',
your father says to the nodding aunts who raise their
glasses, wishing each other 'Good health', 'Many happy
returns', 'A long life together', to the uncles who are
looking out of the window, at the cars, they're trying to
catch the news on the radio, they smoke, laugh, pick up a
volume of an encyclopaedia from the shelf, look up the
names of famous men, read the text beside the photographs
(date of birth, place of birth, what they were, i.e. what
titles they bore (sir, Jesuit, nuclear scientist, statesman,
duke, racing-cyclist), what is known about them, i.e. which
things worth knowing, who has written books about them,
when they died), 'With whom do I have the honour?', you
say, you're standing in a cloud of smoke you hold the glass
in your hand, the room is full of evening dresses, ladies
and gentlemen are smiling, nodding politely, making
conversation, photographers say 'Excuse me - excuse me -',
edging their way amongst the groups, taking a photograph of
two gentlemen shaking hands with each other, two ladies
greeting each other, one gentleman speaking, standing in
a group talking, gesticulating, cracking jokes while the
others frown/look bored/show indifference, he begins to
speak in a low voice (confidentially) while people listen
approvingly: that is how the photograph appears in the
newspaper: he's talking in a low voice (confidentially) while
the others incline their heads towards him (are listening
approvingly), 'Oh yes,' you say, 'Very nice indeed'. Will

he give anything away? Flatter you? Show interest
for the sake of appearances? Will he simply remain
polite? Make no mention of anything? You know that he
knows, your name is being mentioned in the groups, people
look stealthily at you, ladies giggle, gentlemen pretend
indifference, these are all familiar faces. Are they friends?
Enemies? What do they know? How do they know? Who told
them? Who knows what? You can't tell THE LETTERS apart,
the confessions, the disclosures, the admissions, the boasts,
the data, the circumstances, you avoid the photographers,
you distribute photographs. Are you making it difficult?
Complicated? Should you surrender (expose yourself)
defencelessly to the crowd? Should you completely hide
your existence? So that only you yourself know about it,
so that you have no name in the encyclopaedia, no photograph, no curriculum vitae? So that you simply don't exist
or do exist, does a dream exist, a hallucination? You leave
the party, re-read the rough copy of the letters, compare
the expressions, think about the alterations (Do the
alterations occur in yourself? Are they alterations of
expression? Is an alteration of expression an alteration in
yourself?), you weigh the words one against the other:
white/colourless, gravity/need, good/advantageous, bad/
harmful, beautiful/familiar, ugly/strange, war/trade,
machine gun/calculating machine, uniform/publicity, you
weigh them against their readers (weigh the idea you have
of the words against the idea you have of their readers),
you imagine the circumstances in which the letters arrive:
there is a lot of mail, some of the mail has been long
awaited by the addressee, his attention is monopolized by
it, he overlooks your letter (he overlooks the contents (the
idea which you have of the contents)), for instance, you kept
it white on purpose, he finds it colourless, the letter lies
around for a few days, disappears in the waste-paper
basket, or: one had been awaiting the letter, one had
expected that it would be good (advantageous), one is
disappointed (it does not come up to the expectations, one
had thought it would be familiar, but it appears strange),
or: one had been prepared for a tournament of courtesies,
for a network of flatteries, and then one reads an
unambiguous declaration, an inescapable confrontation, an
ultimatum, or: one had imagined the letter to reveal

(confess) a need, for which one might offer help, whereby
one might have an opportunity to give proof of one's
generous heart (one's generosity, one's heart) and then the
letter is only the expression of the absolute gravity of a
situation i.e. of the absolute impossibility to be helped. You
are aware of certain errors, of a wrong (inappropriate) use
of a word, a question of atmosphere, of nuance, never of a
real difference of meaning: to the marshall you use the
word publicity, it doesn't have any meaning to him, he can't
place it in his world, is probably contemptuous of it, so he
doesn't understand it, or: to the industrialist you use the
word uniform, he is suspicious, distrusts your motives,
he is on his guard and further contact isn't possible with
him, or: to the moralist you use the word harmful, he asks
you to enlarge, finds the word misleading, he can't tolerate
it, or: to the politician you use the word bad, he heaps
abuse on you, says that you want to undermine the
revolution/law and order, that you're muddle-headed.
These are all possibilities, this is the probable fate of the
letters, whereby - this is obvious - it is not a question of
facts as such but of their interpretation. Your loneliness is
fundamental, it is inherent, it is unbearable inside the house
you weigh the words, choose the addressees, write the
envelopes, cycle to the post-office, cars zoom by, motor
cyclists swerve past you, they sit bolt upright, drive self-
assuredly and skilfully through the traffic, any car might
hit you, the road is bumpy, the cycle path is narrow beside
the railway, a defect, an absent-mindedness (there are
hundreds of possible defects, hundreds of causes of
absent-mindedness, for instance, someone's eye is caught
by your hat or by your linen trousers which show under
your raincoat like pyjama trousers, or by your raincoat
itself while one is blinded by the sun, your appearance holds
the attention for a moment, it is probably unusual, makes
people momentarily curious), the car turns off the road,
the driver slams the brakes on as hard as possible, the car
skids, the traffic is held up, people stand watching, curious
and without interest, with thumping heart you cycle on,
your hands tremble but your hand keeps clutching the apple,
the green-grocer calls out, people look round at the boy who
is running away past the front gardens, you leap on to a
vacant plot, the nettles sting your legs, you run along the

hedges, stand in the garden shed, panting, the apple is
bruised, the greengrocer talks loudly amongst the crates,
he points out how you were walking past, snatched an apple
away while he shouted and ran and ran, while people were
watching. Do they understand what happened? That they
saw you run away i.e. appear i.e. surprise the neighbourhood, annoy the greengrocer, make him aware of your
passing by, running off? That you will come past again,
at five o'clock when everybody is returning from work? The
greengrocer is busy by the counter, you place a net on it
containing five shiny apples which your auntie Milly gave
you, you run off, cause the man to leave his shop, dumb-
found him, the neighbours, the customers. Does your
auntie Milly suspect who you are? You are folding paper
boats under your grandfather's smiling eye, the sun plays
on the water in the tub, your auntie Milly comes out of the
kitchen holding a basket with five shiny apples, a naughty
boy (a liar, a thief) has pinched one from the greengrocer's,
he ran off past the front gardens, people didn't recognize
him, he disappeared through a vacant plot, you let your
boat down in the water, you are busy building a boat out of
wood, with a screw, worked by elastic, you wind the
screw, the elastic becomes intertwined as it tightens,
becomes a chain of hard knots, the boat shoots forward on
the pond, the boys wait till it falters near the edge, then
they slap their thighs roaring with laughter, the elastic is
unwound, the boat drifts about at the other side of the pond,
you can't swim, you daren't wade through the duckweed, the
boys get hold of you, half a dozen of them are pulling on your
arms and legs, they throw your trousers to each other above
your head, 'Adam!', 'Your fig leaf!', 'We'll tell the
teacher, your dad, your aunts, your grandfather, we'll tell
the dean, your uncle, that you walk around in the woods
without your pants on,' you hide under the sheet, holding
your breath, your father comes rushing up the stairs,
holds you under him, 'I've had enough of it, my boy, you're
not going to spread any more tales about me when the whole
family is present', he spits at you, the house is empty, his
face is red, swollen, close to you, he pushes you down on
your knees, grabs your penis, his breath is everywhere
around you, 'This isn't going to trouble us any longer,'
'This won't put us to shame any longer,' he laughs loudly,

you hear your mother talking in a low voice, disapprovingly,
the bed creaks, he begins to whisper furiously, small
flames hiss in the dark, the rooms downstairs are empty,
the drinks, the cups pushed together in the sink, the ash
trays are full of cigarette ends, the window above the kitchen
door is open, the flames flicker past the photographs, the
street is empty, you're trying to find words for your
letters, words from different ages and continents, you put
them in rows, arrange them according to size, listen to
them, fit them together according to their construction out
of vowels, consonants, syllables, - aggressive words
which defend their factual meaning at the expense of the
things they indicate, you catch them in a context of sweet-
flowing ones, smilingly ambiguous, a hundredfold glittering
and irreplaceable, - indifferent and pale words are absorbed
in festive sounds, you neutralize meanings, you wrap up
statements in rows of doubts, objections are superseded by
facts, facts get lost in arguments, - this you release, you
allow it to be carried around, you move amongst people,
(seemingly) innocently you sit on a stool, smoking, you
find a way to a table, 'Good evening', 'I beg your pardon -
Good evening', 'How are you?' people ask invitingly, 'Very
well, thank you', 'Thank you - Thank you', 'And you?' you
say, stung, this is a trap, they're counting on your good
manners, as long as you join in the game you've got to
admit defeat, 'I'm very well indeed,' the neon light flashes
on and off in the smoke, -indeed-indeed-indeed-, Main
Street, Owls' Drive, you think as you move on, 'How nice
to see you here', 'Very nice to see you too', you've hit that
ball back, he's checkmate, rue de la Commune, ' over
there is a face you cannot avoid, you cannot go past it.
What would happen if you simply moved right through it?
You only need to correct your memory, to think away this
face completely and everything connected with it,
possibilities, facilities, addresses, encounters,... 'Hello.
I'm afraid I'm disturbing you', 'Not really, do sit down,
tell me, how are you', you read that, you think, I'm not
going to kneel (I won't go down on my knees), rue Bonaparte,
Kings Road, rue de la Victoire, you get up, you're getting
ready to go (All the time you're getting ready), but you're
not going, for instance, you don't move towards the
counter, 'Waiter!', some people look round, the waiter

hasn't heard you, the people who look force you to call
out again, more loudly, the waiter looks up absentmindedly, you press far too large a sum in his hand, you
squeeze your way out into the darkness, towards the lamp-
posts, the facades, the water, 'Could I have a word with
you? Your letters have made a deep impression on me, I
would be very pleased if...', you turn away abruptly, you
hurry off to the lavatories, Inselstrasse, you lock yourself
in. How will you get out of here? Will you wait until the
last customers have left, the lights are turned off, the
windows are opened, the chairs are turned upside down on
the tables? Will you climb out of the lavatory? How will you
get out of this shaft, past barred windows with geraniums,
with washing, with dishes of food left out to be kept cool?
How will you get on to the roof? How from the roofs into
the street below? Will you disguise yourself? You tousle
your hair, make stains on your clothes, your shoes are
covered in mud, your tie is badly knotted, it's crumpled,
your collar is unbuttoned, you talk in broad dialect, you
roll a cigarette, let the paper slide past the tip of your
tongue, knock the ends straight on the back of your hand,
with finger and thumb you stick the cigarette between your
lips it hangs down at a slant, 'Hey mate, watch it, hey', you
laugh back awkwardly, ''Ave one on me', you say generously,
you lean on the counter, drink, laugh out loud, swear (you
can swear without swearing, without anyone noticing that
inwardly you are trying to swear really), you make friends,
rave, you look around the cafe, they're sitting at the tables,
stand in clusters arguing, some stand in pairs at the
counter, glance around, hold each other briefly by the
shoulder, the wrist, talk to each other in a muffled voice,
one flicks a speck of dirt from his eye with his little finger
underneath his glasses, no one recognizes you when you look
at them scoffingly.

No one suspects anything.

In the mirror is the open door. In the open door, a little
lower, is the second open door. Between the two light falls
from the left. In the second open door, a little lower, is the
third. Between the second open door and the third, light
falls from the left too. In the third open door, a little lower,
is the fourth. Between the third and the fourth open doors
there is a bundle of light coming from the left. Also the
fifth, sixth, seventh open doors can be distinguished.
(Because THE OPENINGS fit inside each other, they become
smaller and smaller, they become gradually innumerable.)
The relation between two consecutive open doors is always
the same bundles of light become proportionally smaller.
Are they all copies of the first one? Does the distance
between each open door and the one behind it decrease in
the same proportion? Do the spaces between the open doors
therefore gradually become smaller? When the biggest door
is closed, the view is blocked (not removed: because you
saw it once, it comes back before your mind's eye when
you close your eyes). When a door is closed, the view
beyond is blocked. Are there steps behind each open door?
Does one have to jump from each doorstep into the next
space? Is it possible that someone might come towards you
from the space behind the smallest door (Does it exist?)
climbing from one bundle of light into the next? He stands
in front of the mirror, his face is blemished by a rash, the
pores on his nose are blocked, a tiny red vein runs
across his right eye-ball, but his teeth are sound, they
feel pleasant after having been brushed, strings of beads,
bracelets, necklaces hang on the wall by the mirror, bottles
of perfume, jars of make-up stand in a row on the marble
top, the dressing table has been pushed right up against the
wall, he looks through the flap-window - two floors below -
into the girls' washroom they're playing about under the

showers, helping each other to pluck out hairs, comparing
measurements, dressing or undressing, underwear and
outer garments hang from hooks high up at the back, his
skin is brown, his loins are narrow, his penis stands
straight up against his belly, the girls giggle, they're
smoking, he is (actually very) slim, his hands are long, a
girl trips about on high heels, wearing only a woollen
jumper around her shoulders, he stands up, the girl has
tall eyebrows, not one of the girls looks at the flap-window,
yet they are all aware that it's open, they chatter, they
shake with laughter, look in each other's eyes, take each
other by the shoulders, he is amongst them, through the
flap-window he sees you sitting in front of the mirror your
penis stands up straight, there are necklaces, jars, bottles
of perfume, bracelets around you the girls are cupping
their breasts in the palms of their hands while dancing
around him you hold the receiver pressed against your ear
you hear the rustling of silk, she swallows, her tongue
licks her lips, 'I'm stroking my thighs', she whispers,
she pants, the stroking becomes fiercer, brusquely you
put the receiver down, you walk (again) along the street,
some men (gentlemen) are in a hurry, inhale deeply, hold
the butt between thumb and index-finger, throw it in front
of them on the foot-path they crush it with a to-and-fro
turning of their right foot, walk on without seeing anybody,
find their way blindly; women are calmer - chatting,
stopping in front of shop windows looking at their reflections,
pulling the collar of their coat straight holding their right
glove in their gloved hand before their breast, their handbag
hangs across their stomach, the girl crosses the road with
determination, you follow her from by the station you
hoped she might waver, that she might be aimless, a girl
wandering along the streets, looking at the cinemas, sitting
down on a terrace without expecting anyone, buying a
magazine out of boredom, lighting a cigarette; who has no
friends, is unknown in a town where she has plenty of time,
where she knows no one, she enters a telephone booth,
picks up the receiver, talks busily while her eyes look at
nothing, pigeons strut around the booth looking for crumbs,
pellets, she puts the receiver down, takes her handbag,
pushes the door open, looks around, amidst the pigeons,
notices a taxi, beckons, walks a few steps, the car waits

briefly at the traffic lights, she sits in the back looking
through the front window, the lights are green. Several
cafes are already closing, your hotel room is dusty, the
flowered wallpaper is smudged next to the bed, the streets
are depopulated, shops and offices are empty, it is chilly
in the light of the street lamps, you feel light-headed with
sleep surrounds you, you are surrounded, rooms follow one
another, return again and again give the illusion (?) of
moving in a circle, therefore of security (familiarity) of
being accepted in a community is a system, a complex of
conventions, of possibilities for contact (?) without (?)
risks, a complex of identifications which you don't want,
you move from one room into the next, in fact you're never
quite in a room always on the way to another one in which
you are on the way to another one, you do not always move
in the same direction as the hands of a clock, often you turn
back you make overtures possibly you prepare for encounters
instead of walking in the same direction as the others
(eliciting rivalry, victories or defeats), you greet in the
light which enters in bundles as others cross doorsteps they
come towards you in the mirror i. e. they become larger in
relation to you, clearer, bolder, readier. But why does this
perturb you? Why do you get excited about it? You brush
your hand across your forehead, talk with affectation - much
too loudly - into the receiver you move from one ear to the
other, you skin feels greasy, you flicker your eyelids, 'oh
yes' you say, 'I'm very pleased about it but you see the time
the place though', you get stuck in it, you toil with the
greatest effort at a sentence to which you go on adding
clauses in order to finish it you get entangled in ever more
complicated constructions from which you try to disengage
yourself by new additions, the final point moves further and
further away, grammatically the whole thing becomes more
and more doubtful (ly) you stand there, sweating and
stammering, only words can save you, the impulses, the
discoveries which keep reality in control, deduce it, while
rubbing your neck with your right hand you rest first on
one foot then on the other, your left thumb describes circles
on the receiver while Janna (Marina) looks at you derisively
in the mirror you look at Marina (Janna) while you take the
corners you catch up, you remain on the left, your penis
stands up straight, she spreads her knees, closes them,

spreads her knees, closes them, spreads her knees while
you rub circles on the steering wheel, you can't stop, have
your hands free between them have the choice, you can
only get to your destination as fast as possible they are
(stand) facing each other, Janna (Marina) with her smart
boots on, Marina (Janna) has pushed her skirt up, they look
in each other's eyes, stand on either side of the bed, of the
mirror, the chandelier hisses between them the flames
leap, the one moves a step to the right, the other to the
left, they remain opposite each other, turning round the
candles, the needle of the compass moves steadily, the
south changes the position of the north changes the
position of the south, again it's nothing to do with you,
you're simply outside it, an onlooker, a witness, a peeping
tom while they caress their vulvae with their fingertips,
not letting each other go and not seeing only themselves in
each other, the trembling round their lips, the licking of
their tongues, the circles of the slowly turning chandelier,
the 33 candles heat each other, the wax drops on the bed
while they burn more fiercely, slowly growing smaller,
so that the distance between them increases, the spiral
of light turns in the rising air their hands are busy they see
each other only in a blur on the other side, your penis
stands up straight, neither of them has noticed you, the
chain comes away from the ceiling while the bed catches
fire everywhere at once you see (look at) the glow only in
the frame rages a circle of flames you stand in the middle
stand your face, your shoulders, your belly are immovable,
untouched in the tangle, the lapping flames, the shadows
play on your skin, along your lips, your nipples, they
caress, they glide, rage at your back the fire is as great
as the mirror. When will it stop? What is left around you?
The burnt-out room, the walls with the flowered paper
streaked with soot, the iron bedstead with burst springs,
on either side Janna and Marina, standing straight, their
hair is burnt off, their eyes are rigid and mad, their
mouths wide open without lips, with thumb and forefinger
they hold their vulvae open, they crash against the floor
in fragments, the room is an aquarium of soot, you grabble
in their bellies both the embryos are shrivelled blotchily
scorched they hang from the navel cord like from a thread,
they are clappers in cracked bells, you wade through the

soot creeps in your nose, your mouth is dirty and dry,
people come towards you with cameras, with microphones,
asking for explanations, for your findings, men, women,
parents, parents-in-law, grown-up children sit in dark
living-rooms, drinking tea, smoking, someone gets up,
people yawn, you say: 'I can't explain anything, I don't know
any more about it, I've only begun to realize that fundamen-
tally no one knows anything about it, that every attempt to
penetrate is useless, that people are not aware of their
ignorance'. They take it amiss that you say you can't tell
them anything, that you know the others don't know, they
rise from their easy chairs, loosen their ties, turn the
knob, the men talk together for a while, two sentences,
irritably because they were disturbed in their (spiritual)
rest, they work it off again (spit it out) the women haven't
heard it, they fuss about the ashes, about smudges on the
upholstery, turn the bed covers back, it is chilly, the
crucifix, the image of the Virgin Mary (the portrait, the
genre-piece) hangs on the flowered (striped) wall paper, one
turns on one's side, a car goes by, one switches the bedlight
off, waits till the other sleeps, the other waits till the other
sleeps, the alarm clock ticks, it is set for seven o'clock, it
is the start of another day without perspective, the tram, the
memos, the colleagues who have nothing new to say, they
know you (think they know you: there is nothing with which
you can amaze them), you are someone to them who looks
very much like them but is just that little bit inferior, each
of them has something in which they can outshine you (they
think they have something in which they can outshine you),
the same thing in which you outshine them (think you
outshine them), that hidden, as yet unknown something, this
possibility to amaze, in short this possibility, this
expectation of yours, (of each of them) to launch out, to
turn into action, to make true, incontestably, so that you
can smile, envy gives way to pats on the shoulder, interest,
helpfulness, 'Excuse me, gentlemen, someone is waiting
for me', she waves to you, they don't know her, the door of
the car is open, she is wearing a black velvet suit, she
smokes, they see her white lace cuffs, the Byron collar,
her smart boots, 'Have a pleasant weekend, gentlemen,' it
sounds apparently ordinary, with concealed irony you shake
hands with them, they say nothing, they hadn't expected

this, you cross the road diagonally, 'You are very early, Janna', you kiss her on the mouth, she briefly puts her right arm round your shoulders rests her hand with the cigarette, they are level with you on the other side of the street they see her right arm on your back, the back of your head, her hand with the cigarette between index and middle finger, they hear 'You are very early Janna', they look at the strange number plate, you get in, the doors are slammed shut, she starts the engine, you ride in a white sports car past some men, civil servants, they are well-groomed, walk badly, gawkily, (awkwardly), they smoke, carry brief-cases, a few a document-case, they stay behind on the pavement, nod incredulously, they only see your head, your right shoulder, your right hand at the door handle, Janna turns the corner, 'You are very early Janna, ' you crossed the road, 'Excuse me gentlemen, someone is waiting for me', you said good-bye, quite simply, there was nothing special to be seen on your face, you kissed her on the mouth, she put her arm round your shoulder, still holding the cigarette in her hand, her gestures were slow, graceful, she smiled, the doors slammed shut when they were already a few feet ahead of you, none of them looked round (dared look round) they did look sideways when they heard (felt) the car going past you greeted with a smile, quietly, amiably, they nodded incredulously (a little perplexedly it seemed to you), you talked to Janna while you drove the short stretch to the corner, just when the car turned the corner, when you were still visible through the front garden of the corner house, exactly at that moment Janna pulled at her cigarette, turned towards you, smiled about something just between the two of you, there was great intimacy in her look, when they arrived at the corner you had long since turned the next corner, they waited for the tram, four of them got into a car together, (the family car of one of them, kitchen-green with speckled upholstery) they held their brief-cases on their knees, What did they say? What did they guess? Are the four waiting by their car are the others letting trams go by, do their tongues start wagging, do they jump from one assumption to another while you move further and further away from them (become more and more enigmatic to them), are they remembering anecdotes which in their view throw

light on the incident? Do they expect you back on Monday?
Do they imagine you in Switzerland? In Egypt? Do they
dismiss it all with: 'We'll soon see, there's nothing to it'?
The tall girl trips through the washroom, a friend caresses
her lips, they look in each other's eyes, round the mirror
hang necklaces, bracelets, strings of beads, bottles of
perfume, jars of make-up stand in a row on the marble top,
the dressing-table has been pushed against the wall, your
penis stands up straight while two floors below the girls
are playing about, the two of them are sitting on bath
towels by the wall, in the space (?) behind the smallest
door something moves, little doors are closed, little light
bundles vanish, silently it becomes bigger, (comes closer)
the little man climbs from little light bundle into little
light bundle, closing the little doors behind him, the future
(the past) comes ever closer, becomes clearer, (more
frightening), the man slams the doors behind him, he
strides from one light bundle into the next he keeps his
eyes steadily fixed on the mirror, his eyes are hard, he
moves faster and faster, there are another seven open
doors left, another six, five, you keep looking rigidly into
the mirror, the girls know it (feel it). They don't look up.

The door opens (is opened), a lady (woman) stands
opposite a gentleman (man) stands opposite a lady lets him
in, the door is closed, net-curtains hang in front of the windows, blackbirds hop around on the lawn round the house
stands in a garden adjoining other gardens in which are
houses, a car drives slowly along the road amongst the rows
of Japanese cherry trees, here and there stands a dustbin
at the roadside, the neighbour opposite sees a gentleman
coming out of the house, he walks down the path, at the
letterbox he turns round, he waves to the lady who waves
back, the door is shut, a car stops in front of the house,
turns into the gravel drive, a gentleman with raised penis
walks up to the front door, rings the bell, in the mirror of
the lobby he sees himself and the back of the lady (woman)
who kisses him while the neighbour opposite watches from
behind her net curtains the door is closed, neighbouring
children come outside to play, in a room the light is turned
on, one by one the curtains are drawn, blinds are lowered,
the lady comes outside, gets into the car, drives off, a
gentleman comes home (?) greets (nods at) a gentleman
arriving in a car, children run towards him, jump around
him as he walks up the path to the front door A SLIM
YOUNG LADY rings the doorbell, a gentleman (the naked
one?) bows elegantly, the door closes, the ball is hit to
and fro drily (peacefully?) a lady plays tennis with a
gentleman plays tennis with a gentleman plays tennis with
a lady, their dress differs, there is no wind, bigger
children are watching the ball which (the game which) is
kept going between each other (amongst, with each other),
while playing one wins/loses, the slim young lady comes
outside, she gets into her (?) car, waves, you try to
follow her shadow which glides across the sand is uneven in
parts with which at some moments he coincides, you begin

to recognize her contours more and more while she slowly
seems to sink away, the rocking which keeps your eyes
fixed on her belly, on her thighs, on the almost impercep-
tible contraction of her thigh muscles, moves to the upper
part of her body, she holds her arms above her head, she
comes down step by step where there is no door, no
window, no table around which children play, she steadily
descends into the void, remaining at the same level i. e.
the number of treads above her remains the same. Do the
treads move? Does she move? Does she move towards
you? Are you moving yourself while she strikes a few
poses? She crosses her arms, puts her hands on her hips,
raises them behind her head, crouches down looking at
her navel, lays her head in your hands, says nothing,
smiles at you in the camera, but this is an optical illusion,
a delusion, steadily she moves the picture which is held
captured, i. e. is looked at, she has long thighs, the hair
which falls down her shoulders is black, in its shadow you
hardly see her eyes, her lips are parted, there is a
trembling round the sides of her nose, she brings her
fingers together round her lips. Is she touching them?
Does she feel how near they are? The sand isn't sand, it's
the wind which rustles, driving her away from you in
spirals while you try to see who she is who doesn't exist
except in fields of colour, in a play of light and dark,
reactions to the light which outline exactly what cannot be
grasped, is over-clear and enigmatic, smiling and not
looking (not looking at him) she leaves the house, she waves,
gets into her (?) car drives slowly to the main road it merges
into the traffic drives a car amongst cars pull out, catch
up, slow down, drive in a line, leave the main road. Which
car is driving amongst cars? Is it (still/already) amongst
them? Where is it? In the house music is played is hardly
audible in the garden, all doors inside are open, no action,
no thought is possible outside her in the rooms which she
fills more loudly or more mutedly, in the garage, in the
attic, in the lobby she sounds quietly between the white walls
of the living room she is forcefully present she is ear-
shattering in the bedroom lie a man and a woman on the bed,
he/she is naked, she/he is dressed, one of them is smoking
while the other talks, cries, caresses, one follows the
circles which spiral upwards to the ceiling is white lies the

sheet of paper on the table, one writes a signature, a
second time it differs from the first time, a third, fourth,
fifth time one writes the same signature differs three,
four, five times from itself. What is itself? What deviates
(differs)? To what extent are differences permitted i.e.
valid i.e. the signature is recognizable amongst other men/
women are attractive/repulsive/uninteresting/charming
she lies beside him lies another lies beside another makes
love to her in the room in which he lies on her lies a
familiar body makes familiar movements are the same and
differ from the one to the other smiles, cries argues,
turns away from the music which is everywhere, he/she
goes to the garage, to the lobby, to the garden is quiet and
dark, a breeze makes the leaves flutter, the tennis court is
deserted he/she stands in the garden you can't spend the
night on a marble pedestal stands a bronze man looks left/
right in the direction of his left arm is stretched out
(commands, wards off, greets, points...) in the
continuation of his right upper arm, his right lower arm
goes up diagonally to the hand is at the level of his eyes are
hollows through which you can look into the man. Is he
empty? In the right hand there is a hollow between the palm
and the fingers he holds (hides) something/nothing moves
on him, he rests on his left leg is in profile the foot points
in the direction of the arm, the right heel is lifted, resting
on his toes he holds (keeps) himself in balance (balanced)
the body is built as a show-piece of beauty and strength
(rest and strength) radiate from it from the hollows of the
eyes and the right hand's hollows are hollows. Does a
cord leave from the brain? Does a clapper hang in his
chest? Can one hear the wavering (the insecurity, the
exhaustion, the powerlessness) as a soft (melodious)
tinkling (singing) which comes out of the eyes? Does a
bird chirp in the right hand? Is he Zeus? Poseidon?
Neither? If he is both, what difference is there between
them then? (How can they be distinguished?) How long has
he (have they) been standing there immovably (unchangeably)
in this posture which announces an action (a deed) which
doesn't take place, as if it existed in the announcement (the
appearance) of itself? Does he (do they) exist only in the
eyes which see him (them) i.e. every moment anew (therefore differently)? The rhythm changes with the melody

changes with the rhythm underlines the melody blossoms
out of the rhythm is melody is rhythm and melody are
inseparable (cannot be separated from each other) a man
and a woman copulate on the bed a man copulates with
another woman copulates with another man copulates with
a woman leaves the house, the blinds are down, she waves
from the car, the door is closed, the rooms bathe in light,
on tables, on cupboards there are bouquets, the man walks
from one room into the next, he looks at the bed in the
mirror it is a white field without dimensions are those of
the frame round the mirror is made of gold is the melody
which sounds from the rhythm glistens in the mirrors, in
the portraits, in the china on a tray on the table, the
teapot, the cup still half full, the other one has a rim of
lipstick, cigarettes stick out of a packet, the cocktail
cabinet is open, on the main road drives a lady, she turns
into a side road, pulls up in front of a villa, rings the
doorbell, in the mirror of the lobby she sees herself and
the back of the gentleman who kisses her. Does he kiss
her? He kisses a young lady who unbuttons her coat which
he puts away, they exchange a few words, they sit in the
living-room together. Who sits with whom in the living
room? She sees him get an erection, she undresses while
he undresses, he chases her through the rooms (She lets
him chase her. Does she let him chase her?), in the mirror
she sees his head and his back moves above a panting woman
tosses under a man above her who moves up and down moves
a back in the mirror has a golden frame gleams in the light
like gold which gleams in the light comes from the lamp
which burns gives light makes a golden frame gleam in a
room where two people are copulating, in an empty room
(the bed is made, there is no one at home), in a room where
two people make each other ill (a woman cries, calls, kicks,
a man overturns a chair, tears the net curtains, the slats of
the blinds are not painted, he walks out of the room), he
stands in the garden there is no wind, a breeze makes the
leaves flutter, the camera moves with the view which
changes, is transformed, shifts and remains the same (?)
view because the same camera holds it in its field of view
the man imagines that he keeps her in this picture which he
steadily keeps in view in which a young woman walks
(away), smiles, cries, turns her face away, sleeps while

he views her i.e. views himself i.e. makes actions out of
movements, words become meanings (symbols) change with
the context, the intonation, the circumstances change with
the words are a source of doubts, guesses, interpretations
change with the context, the intonation, the circumstances
bring a man in contact with a woman responds/does not
respond to the man responds/does not respond to the
woman stands in front of the fire rages between her legs
are eerily lit she laughs and rocks i.e. she rocks the fire,
the shadows glide between two positions (views) which are
each other's counterpart, your eyes follow the steady
approach (retreat) of an end position (initial position) which
isn't one because she really describes a circle, a figure
without starting points (points of contact) you see her
laughing heartily, the flames leap, you hear nothing, these
are views from a film, photos on which you can put your
signature on each photo there is the same, all photos
differ just like all signatures are the same and differ.
Where is she? The fire blazes freely and aimlessly it
consumes itself while the night slips by, seed dries up,
forms hard patches on the sheet lie little hairs, he picks
up the long black ones, puts them on a white sheet of
paper lie a few long black hairs curl a little, he moves
them, tries to bend them, fold them, the parts which are
not flat on the paper cast thin little shadows make the
opposite movements of the hairs are long black hairs are
long black hair has the woman who opens the door for a
gentleman (man) who is (dressed like) a cousin enters the
house, in the house opposite the neighbour goes on with her
work, a (the) car stands under a Japanese cherry tree
which stands by the path leading to the front door out of
which comes a slim young lady reaches the main road at
a point from where a car follows her steadily drives
behind her (from where she notices a car which keeps
behind her), she drives fast and with ease while following
the car with the gentleman (man) in the mirror who follows
her (drives behind her) she catches up, slows down, turns
into a side road, stops, she enters a villa, a blackbird
hops on the lawn is closely cut, no light can be seen through
the slats of the blinds are painted white like the whole
house.

Through the net curtains the light falls in the room sits a
man amongst the patches of sun on carpets, armchairs,
cupboards, walls shift imperceptibly shifts time the man
eats by a table on the bed he reads walking from one room
into the next he peers through the net curtains he sees the
ladies smoking hanging (?) in their COFFINS in the nearby gardens glistens the glass between which they lie their
heads leaning on one arm leans on the glass/on the air leans
on nothing moves (happens) in the gardens play children are
jumping under the coffins just cannot reach them, they call
their mummy hears them/doesn't hear them lying with one
leg drawn up, vulvae like fleshy leaves are on display the
ladies smile in all directions where villas, lawn, children
and ladies are on both sides of the road where cars drive
up to the corner there they wait to turn into the main road
they change into first gear a car drives on the gravel
crunch footsteps move away from the house (from the man)
peers while the gentlemen play tennis behind the gardens
tick-tock the tennis balls dart to and fro dart invitations
(flatteries), compliments (responsibilities), civilities
(attacks) cannot touch the ladies while they smile they
rest their head on one hand lies on one knee rests on
nothing. Can one imagine a gentleman jumping under a
glass coffin (under a lady)? takes on various shapes
(dimensions) (exists in various shapes (dimensions)), is
various shapes (dimensions) behind the concave/convex
glass swell her thighs shrink her breasts stretch her lips
(her smile) while he walks from window to window he
compares the continual changing (the changing continually).
What then does he see, the change (the succession) of his
points of view through the undulations in the glass
changing from point of view to point of view (from
gentleman to gentleman, from lady to lady) changing

feelings, reflections, expectations alter in the course of
the game bores one (one loses)/one is absorbed (one wins)/
one plays on grimly (one stakes everything in order (yet)
to win) while smiling the ladies stand in the driveways the
bigger and smaller (more expensive and cheaper) cars
in which the gentlemen come/coming home greet each
other (nodding/uttering a commonplace). Do they see the
man as he comes out? Does he put his hands in his trouser
pockets does he look self-possessed/full of purpose is the
mark of a man (is that by which one knows/recognizes) a
man who looks around the garden at the hedges, the flower
beds, the walls with the windows in which the hedges, the
flower beds are reflected against the net curtains behind
which he looks at the ladies he greets amiably (apparently)
without noticing their nakedness (their stately obscenity) he
moves further on he stands in front of the glass-concrete
slabs are transparent his (shadow) image falls on the car
drives backward out of the gate is closed by a gentleman/ a
slim young woman drives slowly up to the corner the car
disappears on the main road. What do the others see? a
gentleman trying to look in through the net curtains (tries
whether he (one) can look through the net curtains) into the
rooms with armchairs, lamps, tables, carpets, pictures
other than (differing from, distinguished from) rooms
with armchairs, lamps, tables, pictures are alive (are
present) in dimmed light penetrates the tick-tocking which
the ladies follow all day without taking part (without coming
out of their coffins) it gives their smile (their self-
satisfaction, their prudish vanity) the knowledge that the
gentlemen cannot do without them (without their
competition) is healthy (infectious) i. e. keeps the balance
between winning and losing one keeps one's position (one's
dignity, one's worth) considers (feels) oneself affected/
unaffected when (the) others can look in they form a judg-
ment is (sounds) favourable/unfavourable (appreciative (ly)/
disparagingly (ly)) the ball is bounced from one to the other
watched by the ladies, proudly on display in their aquarium
of smoke (of illusions, of hallucinations) can hardly move
about, cannot afford any freedom of movement except in the
undulations of the glass they are themselves they are never
in each other's presence (visibility) is distinguishability. (In
what) do they distinguish themselves from each other? Do

the villas, the gardens, the cars by which the gentlemen
(might want to be able to) distinguish themselves from each
other (might want to be able to) go one better than the other
is the slim young woman driving in and out of the gates,
walking through the garden, arousing the jealousy of the
ladies as she walks in a strapless dress to the car a (the)
man looks in as she leaves the whole neighbourhood looks
at a (the) slim young woman with hair down to the
shoulders in a (the) white sports car drives off/comes
home waits a (the) man sees her walking in the garden
greeting neighbours greet politely (reservedly) greeting
gentlemen interrupt their game while she turns away she
sees (feels) everybody watching i. e. not understanding
(unable to understand) becoming fascinated by a (this) slim
young woman who lives with a (this) man in a (this) villa
lives a (this) (wedded) couple is truly wedded (in wedlock)
unwedded (out of wedlock) are concepts with which one
cannot (in this case) get any further (more) the tongues
begin to wag suppositions (suspicions) fast living binds these
two together probably, certainly, undoubtedly the woman of
this man is an other is the man of this woman does not
display herself (dares not display herself/cannot be a
showpiece) i. e. one doesn't know whether she is there/is
not there, where she is/is not in the house around which
(in which?) nothing ever happens i. e. something happens
which doesn't happen elsewhere, (can (may) happen)
imagining oneself in this villa does the lady/the gentleman
go in and out drives the lady/the gentleman with a/the
gentleman with a / the lady catches up on the main road in
a moment one catches up catching up one is caught up by
him/ her / them. Are there no children? are a burden
trample on the carpet i. e. on the heart (on preconceptions,
on cherished expectations) they seek find preconceptions,
cherished expectations differ from preconceptions,
cherished expectations are connected with age cannot be
handed down/given away/giving makes poorer i. e. richer
i. e. older (old-fashioned) snow-whites and maria gorettis
turned sour lie in state (exalted) above shouting dwarves and
cherubs chase each other amongst the flower beds flowering
/withering is temporarily (alternately) to win/to lose the
(often elderly) princes their (only) goal is to win no other
goal but to win is to win is to be stronger/smarter/cleverer

than the other is to be stronger/smarter/cleverer than the
children break down/ build up what one has built up/broken
down so that nothing grows or fades away while the children
grow one fades away one never acquires what one has not
got someone else walks with a slim young woman in the
garden is bounded by green is reflected in the windows are
closed off by net curtains let through a muted light shines
in rooms where a (this) man and a (this) slim young woman
caress/exasperate/abuse/kick/seek/passionately love
each other looking in each other's eyes they come out of
the garden are alone all eyes on them see a (this) man
together with a (this) slim young woman is all they see
closed net curtains, doors, smoke (from an open fire?) a
high gable roof on which a blackbird is hopping on the
ridge sit two pigeons fly into a tree they disappear (again)
through the door by the terrace lies empty in the sun falls
in bundles through the glass-concrete slabs the car drives out
of the garage doors close. Who is in the car i.e. who is in
the house? is he (perhaps) waiting for her who catches up
on the main road in a moment a slim young woman in a
strapless dress is (perhaps, probably, certainly) not a
dress is a dream in a sportscar white like lightning makes
the traffic move faster go the cars chasing each other are
the (gentle) men smoking nervously at the wheel one is a
number in a queue crossing oncoming cars are numbers
in a queue crossing oncoming cars hamper the view
hampers one's catching up would (perhaps, probably,
certainly) be no catch.

A (the) room is in the house is in the garden which is
between gardens is the room is an image in the mind of
the neighbours think (imagine) a round room of glass (of
light, of shadow) is inaccessible i.e. the man is shut in an
imaginary space evokes an imaginary man who thinks in
images of shadow (of light, of glass) are symbols signify
senses in sentences from sentences is born a space is
round like a man bending over who is inaccessibly shut up
in himself writes i.e. reads i.e. writes on a glass table
i.e. not legibly (not writably)-ility is a question of
moments are places are situations are controlled by
sentences are controlled (are made) in the illusion (the
expectation) of the control of situations drive a man into
a room. A vacuum offers no support (no anchorage) i.e. no
law of gravity keeps the man on the ground he doesn't touch
anywhere has no points of contact with reality does not
act upon him in actions he manifests neither gain nor loss
divide the time is eternity is an indivisible moment is a
sentence is a page is a book is a page is a sentence makes
sense in a moment (makes sense for a moment) is senseless
in reality is the division (interruption) of moments
(eternities) in points of time succeed each other dissolve
them. Has he no contact with reality (with the world
outside)? is steady change is the only (possible) definition
does not relate to the illusion of the man bears no relation
to reality (to the world outside) looks down on/looks up at
i.e. is elsewhere is under or/and above the wires inter-
mingle cross each other form webs are taut in the air make
nothing out of air is wind is movement continues into the
room the sand waves i.e. the water i.e. the sand sinks away
in the water is sucked up by the sand hampers the view of
the man is not visible is he the victim of vibrations go
through him wires form webs are taut in him he works at

a hollow space of air within himself he makes a husk (an
outline) of air in (the) air.

If one ties a knot in a piece of string i. e. the conversation
is resumed in the bustle one pulls the loop tight (er) the
ends come close(r) together the knot is untied (unravelled)
one unravels the tangled skein (the tension/the friction)
i. e. the distance increases between the ends turn and
twist round fingers make A LOOP is pulled tighter with
both hands clutch each other become enmeshed bits of
string accumulate a knot is added to the next one the
untying of the one hinders the untying of the other one the
other the last one i. e. the string has been all tied up the
ends stick out like feelers on either side of the ball rolls
between fingers touch the harder/looser feeling (nerve)
knots are formed from a length of string in two hands
pluck at a piece of string is a sufficient reason/pretext/
possibility for untying is tying is untying is pointless(ly)
being busy is having a purpose which is not quite knowable
(nameable) is behind the horizon is 'felt' by the finger'
tips move in varying i. e. the same ways the string is the
instrument of two forces (contrasts) which react to each
other i. e. are visible to be visible is to be present in
the eyes of the other is in one's own eyes in the eyes of
the other are tendencies/attempts/expectations continue
usually as long as one has a piece of string in one's
hands one has ten, twenty, a hundred threads make a knot
is untied ten, twenty, a hundred times is repeated what
occurs ten, twenty, a hundred times at the same time and
in the same way i. e. (in)visibly in repetitions the tying/
untying frays the string (the connection) i. e. the loops
multiply while a knot is made a knot makes ten, twenty, a
hundred knots make a ten-, twenty-, hundred-fold
simultaneity is (im)possible is ten, twenty, a hundred times
the string is entangled between ten fingers fumble at a
little ball leads with greater difficulty to a string leads with
greater difficulty to a little ball as the uniformity de-creases
in-creases the quantity in circumstances change on the one
hand leads to the other hand leads to the one hand one
wants (?) a piece of string on the other hand one wants (?)
a little ball simultaneously with a piece of string
simultaneously with a little ball is on the way to a piece of

string is on the way to a little ball are ten fingers (in an immovable place) on the way from one to the other except in the form i.e. the content is the form of the (gradually unravelling) piece of string forms the (life) goal of ten fingers form the (life) goal of two eyes form the (life) goal of a moving (on the spot) mind 'feels' a goal is just beyond the horizon blocks the goal is a circle just beyond the horizon comes closer comes the goal is horizon-tal i.e. it expands in (un)wearying dreams intensify as the horizon comes closer to the other comes closer to the one is tied up inextricably with the other.

The man as he sits there i.e. as the neighbours imagine him sitting in the room which they imagine in the villa which they see him walking in his garden walks a slim young woman knows what they guess what she knows that he is not where he is in the round room an outline of air as he sits there at a glass table one gets knocked/shocked without knowing against what/by what one is knocked/ shocked one no longer bothers about the images of shadow (of light, of glass) which are inexplicable (whose cause one cannot find) in the man (whom) one does not see as he succeeds (as one believes he succeeds) in his attempt consists of existing without leading an (the) existence of a man who walks in his garden, plays tennis, comes home by car while children run towards him his wife awaits (him) smilingly his kiss is a formality is his life he (ful)fills. What does he fulfil? his duty is his dignity i.e. he greets condescendingly, he looks down on (looks(perhaps as a result) up at) the man who inaccessibly bent in on (over) himself does things which he doesn't do i.e. which one does not see (which are not visible) and so one suspects a space which is filled by someone who does not fill it (try to fill it) except in the imagination with images of shadows (of light, of glass) manifest the thinking of the man is (appears to be) an illusion (something which has no contact with reality, does not (directly) belong to it) of the man is a hallucination of the neighbours see between the gardens a garden in which stands a villa which is distinguished by net-curtains.

Bundles of light through the glass-concrete tiles on to the
car is droning in the locked garage two dustbins next to two
bicycles against a white-washed wall hangs a radiator behind
logs are neatly stacked up to the level of the roof of the car
is not far from the ceiling of the garage is under the house
stands in the sun on the grass stand villas in two rows form
a straight road is deserted (alone) is a woman staring at a
point on the white-washed wall in front of the car is not
plastered one sees the stacked bricks up to the ceiling
the smoke is immovable and grey she sits behind the
steering wheel gleams in the sun glitter her rings and her
watch indicates the time (the hour) while the engine drones
on the winding road she catches up in a moment she is lost
out of sight hallucination of on-coming cars pull out for a
young woman wears her hair down to her shoulders are
naked so that the whole woman is naked in the imagination
of the on-comers runs away with them the corpse seems
filled with exhaust fumes accumulate in the garage nothing
happens in the rooms a man lies trussed up in front of the
window a car goes by passes a lady calls children play
opposite a garage door is open, a gentleman comes home. Is
the television starting? broadcasting an eye-witness report
of a fire caused the death of victims are carried on
stretchers outside nothing is seen of what can be seen in the
house sits a young woman in the droning car in the garage
is underneath the bedroom where a man sits trussed up
behind the net curtains staring in the sunlight draws lace
work (a mesh) on the walls are a stack of bricks are the
villas in which neighbours eat, watch television, they
copulate at the weekends when the children sleep they
exchange a few words about the children go to school
demands (kills) much time is money is a perpetual worry
makes the ladies smile when they come outside the one can

see i. e. judge the other. The droning can't be heard in
the road, before it is noticed (before an irregularity, an
abnormality is established/is thought to be established) it
will be weeks the grass grows, the letterbox will be
stuffed with letters, cards, folders invite, warn, remind,
thank (contain words of thanks), inform (notify), greet
(contain a cordial, friendly, respectful greeting i. e. the
sender is making a great (grand) journey/is proud of his
prosperity/feels lonely), one enters rooms with pictures
consist of lines cross each other in the picture itself one
sees relationships (tensions) are continued in the rooms
one searches in drawers and cupboards there are papers,
letters, diaries, clippings contain confirmations/denials
(explanations) contradict each other apparent confusion
one seeks arguments i. e. one starts from a presupposition/
an intuitive urge/ a pre-monition guides the investigation
consists of comparing fingerprints are present in the car
sits A ROTTING CORPSE /in women's clothes spread a foul
smell is in the garage fall bundles of sun through the
glass-concrete tiles are transparent are photographs when
one holds them against the light one holds negatives with a
naked young woman in a sportscar is the dream of every
motorist looks up when she drives past she catches up in a
moment one catches up/is caught up/catches up with
others who catch up with others, the speed of the traffic
increases the tension mounts while she goes on catching up
she leaves the catchers-up behind her mutual rivalry hounds
the motorists on while she calmly (?) turns into the side-
road no one is behind her the cars rush past on the main
road the rush goes on at the gravel drive she stops. She
calls out a name in the rooms she walks hurriedly pulls
drawers open in which she looks for letters, documents
are untouched dining chairs and easy chairs stand round
tables stand under lamps hang from ceilings are painted
white is the whole house in which one sees here and there
a fly, a gnat, a moth, crawling, in the lobby buzzes a
wasp flies through the open door she walks into the bedroom
a man lies trussed up in front of the window she stops to
look at the street where children play around the neighbours
(ladies) are exchanging friendly politenesses, she steps
backwards through the man's head lies on the floor she
picks up something from the carpet from his chest rises

and falls heavily, he looks red like blood. Does she
not see, feel, hear him? Is he not there? Why does she
not stumble over him who she thinks has gone away (has left
her) without a note/an explanation/a thank you/an apology/
an accusation/a promise she searches in books, in
clothes, in vases while pressing her heels in his hands he
tries to push away the gag with his tongue, he twists his
arms and legs bleed with the ropes in which she stands
(irresolutely), ropes wind round her ankles. Does he
not feel it? Does he not see and hear her as he lies there
shouting and kicking under (in) a (film of) dream/vacuum
makes her gasp(ing) for breath she runs to the garage run
the policemen find the sportscar gleams in the sunlight
sits a corpse rotting in women's clothes are carefully
taken off, removed like broken flowerpots stand inside
each other on the dustbins beside the car they put a
stretcher with a big plastic cover is held open for the
(police) photographer takes pictures of the situation is
carefully ascertained i.e. certain things stand (more than
others) in the light falls in bundles on the empty back seat
behind the steering wheel it describes lace work (a mesh)
in the room where the man lies/does not lie they keep
walking stepping on his mouth, in his belly while they do not
touch(?) him/while they are not touched they seek
fruitlessly wondering what has happened here i.e. what
caused this situation one seeks in seed stains on a towel is
a bundle of white paper is being written all over with statements of what is being observed in the house (thought to
be observed) goes from mouth to mouth information is
passed on i.e. altered, made different, by someone
different. Motorists have seen a/the young woman (with)
naked (shoulders) in the sportscar catches up in a moment
is caught up they drive more angrily they drive more
recklessly they drive faster without (still) being able to
see her/having seen her/going to see her from a
collective imagination (wish dream) makes the traffic
unsafe (uncertain) is love is impersonal (blind) and
personal (directed to a person/to persons) try to be together
e.g. in a villa with dining chairs, easy chairs, a bed,
pictures at which one looks i.e. one compares i.e. one
judges the photographs one takes regularly in order to
record situations/perpetuate them/remember them. What

do the neighbours remember of this couple (what do they
think they know, what impressions did they have of them)?
Of the man? Of the woman? Of their relationship to each
other? To others? Bundles of light fall through the glass-
concrete tiles on to the car, on the radiator, on the
dustbins are broken flowerpots beside the logs are neatly
stacked against the white-washed wall lean two worn car
tyres. In the rooms crawls here and there a fly, a gnat,
a moth along the walls, by the windows buzzes a wasp.
When has one has the woman last seen the man?

A gentleman/ a lady notices a lady/ a gentleman, who
notices him/her, walks towards him/her, their paths are
going to cross, they smile, the gentleman/the lady holds
out a hand to the hand which is held out in the bustle two
people have for one moment in A HANDSHAKE (physical)
contact is visible to the eyes smile, they see (look at) each
other one moment long (a long moment), passers-by walk
past them, a little group is standing at a tram stop, they
notice/they don't notice, briefly size up the lady, her suit
is blue, she wears her hair down to her shoulders, the
gentleman is gallant, it is clear they are exchanging
friendly words (courtesies). Have they got anything to do
with each other? Who held out his hand first? Did they
shake each other's hand? He notices her, he recognizes
her from photographs and descriptions she recognizes
him, they (hardly) can (wish to) avoid each other, in her
eyes he sees a hesitation she sees vanish from his eyes,
they smile, each holds out a hand at the moment their
hands touch each other they touch a hand which someone
(also) touches (which has got something to do with someone)
which they (also) touch (with which they have got something
to do), they form a circle of touches (contacts) which occur
outside them accidental (?) encounters like this one are
occasions, they sit on a terrace together, strings of people
go past the afternoon passes in a tension between reserve
and spontaneity, he/she rings him/her up, they sit
together on a terrace talking about the others who sit on the
terrace talking about them, about the handshake (the
encounter) and the afternoon on a terrace in town people
walk past each other, recognize faces, greet (nod), evade
looks (contacts) betray your disposition towards the other,
you (hardly) look at her/him, you look her/him straight
in the eyes, you look her/him steadily in the eyes, while

you talk to her/him in a restrained tone, you bend over
towards her/him, strings of passers-by go past, ladies,
mothers, gentlemen, fathers walk past a terrace where a
gentleman and a lady on another terrace the same passers-
by walk past. Does one of them see the (a) connection
between these four people (between these two conversations)?
Here is discussed what is discussed there what is
discussed here i.e. they talk about the other two, about
each of them separately, about their relation to each other,
each talks of his relation to each of the other two is
analysed, subdivided into facts/character traits/
intentions are subdivided into moments/moods/situations
are subdivided into causes/forms of appearance/consequen-
ces are discussed i.e. interpreted i.e. one talks exclusively
of oneself while naming the other (while applying names to
the other), one puts him/her in a framework of names
(assessments) which one offers to one's partner (listener)
(presents to him/her), one does not cease (one urges, one
specifies: becomes confidential) the person (the object) in
question is scattered in ever tinier fragments in the
opinions (prejudices) of the other, the picture gradually
becomes (more) (un)surveyable, vaguer and more familiar,
more unchangeable as less remains unknown (undivided), as
the undivided (uninterpreted) diminishes the actual person is
withdrawn from sight (from objectivity (perception)), one
rambles on, the road is clear for uncontrollable inaccuracies
(untruths) one does not avoid them, one does not avoid him/
her, one shakes hands with someone who shakes hands with
someone whose hand one shakes sits with someone on a
terrace talking about someone who sits talking on a terrace
amongst elderly ladies and gentlemen watching the passers-
by, glancing aside at a gentleman and a lady who are
engaged in lively conversation. Do they catch the words?
Fragments of sentences? Have they sized up the situation?
Are there familiar faces there? He/she pretends not to
have noticed anything, calmly goes on smoking, looks
(seemingly) (fascinated) in another direction, through the
window in which the two are talking, she smiles, he argues,
her handbag stands on a chair between them, white gloves
lie on top of it, every now and then he pushes his glasses
back, rubs a pimple on his left temple, feels at it with his
nail, apparently checks himself from picking at it, picks

at it only briefly, looks at his finger tip, picks at it
briefly, pulls at his cigarette, she talks in a subdued,
emphatic tone, one can tell (it is clear) she is putting
things straight, she puts opinions opposite his, he picks,
looks at his finger, picks, looks at his finger, takes his
handkerchief while going on looking at her (interestedly) he
dabs the blood from his forehead, keeps the handkerchief
pressed against it, looks at his handkerchief, (looks at the
dots of blood), he puts the handkerchief away, she stands
up whereupon (so that) he stands up, he follows her between
the chairs on the pavement they go past the terrace (their
conversation), they exchange a few words (courtesies), they
shake hands in the bustle a handshake brings for one moment
(physical) contact is visible to the eyes smile while they go
in different directions he feels the handshake on his right
hand, he holds it beside his left one, the backs are brown,
hairy, the palms are rosy, the other one lets his glass
of whisky sway, he leans with his elbows on the bar, the
palm of his right hand is rosy, on his little finger is a ring,
the back of his left hand is brown, hairy, he stubs out his
cigarette in the ashtray, you put your right hand on your
left, the right little finger lies on the left thumb, the right
ring finger lies on the left index finger, the middle fingers
lie on each other, the right index finger lies on the left ring
finger, the right thumb lies on the left little finger, the
conversation which you keep going between you and him is a
conversation with the lady beside him is talking with the
lady beside you is talking with him while he talks with you,
he smiles, the rosy fingertips caress the vulvae which your
rosy fingertips (sometimes) hold open while he drinks you
exchange a brief glance with the lady who is leaning against
him, he puts his left arm round her neck, she wears her
hair down to her shoulders, when you put the palms of your
hands against one another /when you put the backs of your
hands against one another they are each other's reflection,
they serve no purpose (are tied, pray), a right and a left
hand cannot replace two right hands/two left hands, two
right hands/two left hands cannot belong to the same man/
woman, a man/woman cannot do what two men/women can
do only what two men/women can do as long as both play
the game, alternate (complement) each other in the actions
which unite/polarize them almost on the corner of a street

two gentlemen/ladies meet each other, they see the other
hesitate, they cannot avoid each other, they sit on a terrace
while two ladies/gentlemen make each other's (further,
personal) acquaintance on a terrace where fathers,
teenagers, tourists pass by, one looks at two dancing
couples on the right of the stage carrying out movements in
a hallucinatory shadow-play accompanies the movements of
a dancing couple on the left of the stage is identical to the
right, they exchange partners, the ballerinas on the left
carry out the opposite (the same) movements as the male
dancers on the right exchange partners (the ballerinas
exchange partners), the couple which danced on the right
dances on the left danced the couple which dances on the right
dances the dancer of the left with the ballerina who danced
on the right with the dancer who dances on the left with the
ballerina of the left dances with the dancer of the right
dances the ballerina of the right towards the left of the
stage, the male dancers have black hair, they are slim and
robust, the ballerinas pirouette, they wear their hair in a
coil, perhaps down to the shoulders, the audience look from
one to the other. Do they see the two couples at the same
time? Does the one differ from the other (the movements
of their counterparts, the one dancer/ballerina from the
other)? Can they exist without differing from each other
i.e. can they stand in contrast to each other/complement
each other? These identical (double) movements are
therefore a delusion i.e. the one moves differently from
the other moves differently from the one the audience
think is better than the other the audience think is worse
than the one feels weaker than (inferior to) the other feels
stronger than (superior to) the one. What do the
ballerinas/the dancers think? What does the one think?
The other? The overtones remain (as) light while the smoke
thickens in the bar where four people (two gentlemen, two
ladies) drink whisky, coats hang in the cloakroom, the
gentlemen pay in turn i.e. the ladies are paid for in turns
by the one gentleman and the other talk about the performance
at which two dancing couples carried out the same movements
simultaneously, the difference between the dancers/
ballerinas lay therefore exclusively in the strength (degree)
of their art depends on the yard-sticks which are used
differ from the one to the other e.g. one attaches

importance mainly to suppleness (ease, superficiality), or
one looks in the first place for the sensitivity (the personal
rhythm) of the dancer/ballerina which sometimes deviates
from the music, which as it were interprets (experiences)
the music (the theme), or one puts teamwork first and
foremost, how well they are attuned to each other, one
looks at two people as if they were one, as one looks at the
right and left hand of the same person are each other's
reflection when one holds the backs/the palms against each
other, a gentleman puts the palm of his right hand on the
back of the right hand of a gentleman standing in front of
him, he stands with his stomach against his back, puts
the palm of the left hand on the back of the left hand of the
other has a short neck on which he breathes, neither of
the two gentlemen is privileged above the other except
in certain respects which keep each other in equilibrium
(are of equal value) just as the gentlemen themselves
while the ladies tear each other's hair, kick, bite, spit
in each other's face, pull and tug at the gentlemen who
keep each other under control, the one clasps with his
hands the hands of the other clasps with his legs the legs
of the one, the ladies make the two totter (freeing them
from each other), they try to unbutton clothes, to pull
them off, two men and two women lie floundering between
the chairs, curse, roar with laughter, the room is full of
smoke round mouths, eyes, hands hardly differ from each
other, a hand with a ring pulls a hand without a ring away
from a screaming woman lies beside a screaming woman
pulls a man towards her who pulls a woman towards him
who kisses a man (gentleman) on a terrace, he wears a
ring on the little finger of his right hand, he smiles, the
lady wears her hair down to her shoulders, they talk about
a gentleman who sits on a terrace with a lady who wears
her hair down to her shoulders, these gentlemen know each
other personally just as the ladies know each other
personally, just as the lady on the one terrace knows the
gentleman on the other and the lady on the other terrace
knows the gentleman on the one, and the other way round.

You cannot see the doorway, a group of men are standing
close together on the doorstep, with their hands in their
pockets they look over each other's shoulders, 'Look where
you're going.' you have to walk more slowly, pretend
you're out for a stroll, you're a gentleman in a noisy
shopping street the meat lies on marble slabs lie red clumps
are woven towards a central point (from a central point
outwards), the blood drips on the slabs, runs across the
veins, small stains and splashes on the long aprons of the
butchers who are smoking, watching the passers-by with
their arms on their back, a little group of them shuffle
into a cafe, their forearms bare, a gentleman is wearing
glasses, black gloves, the butcher's shops are open at the
front, there are tall mirrors on either side, the room on a
cable way above THE STREET might break down, you land
amongst the meat, people crowd around you, the police
force their way towards you, you've got to get away from
here as fast as you can, the money is on the mantlepiece,
she can get dressed, you fumble for your wallet, you
mustn't forget anything, the room sways at the top of the
stairs, on the pavement a group of men are smoking, hands
in their pockets, three girls are waiting at the entrance
to a narrow alleyway, they don't look at the men, stand
around chatting, carrying handbags, smoking, one man
walks on, two men come forward, crane their necks, the
group blocks the pavement, woman have to walk round, the
alley is dimly lit, it winds, you can't distinguish anything
clearly behind the girls, the tallest girl smiles at you,
she throws her cigarette end in front of her on the ground
she stubs it out with the toe of her shoe, 'Excuse me', a
gentleman stumbles, a few men step aside, surprised, you
sidle your way between two girls, the alley is draughty,
dustbins are standing side by side and piled on top of each

other in the yard there is washing hanging on every side,
there is a sickly odour of meat, sides, saddles hang
from big hooks, you follow her up a staircase, turn, pass
doors, turn, pass doors, turn, pass doors, at every tread
you step lower, becoming clearer to the group standing in
the street, to the women, the butchers, the policemen are
watching you as you come down, step by step, with gloves,
your glasses, your ring you carefully put on top of your
trousers, 'Come', she laughs, she sits astride on the
bidet, you don't feel up to much, 'You're not up to much,
are you,' she laughs, the electric heater glows in the
mirrors on both sides, you sweat, a gentleman sits in a
corner seat in the third row (the seats aren't numbered,
anyone wanting to sit in the front with his knees against the
stage will have to hurry), a few (gentle)men are standing
by the wall, they are smoking, standing close together they
fumble for their money, the cashier at the back closes the
curtain, le palais mauresque is full of middle-aged gentlemen with glasses, with hats on top of their overcoats on
their knees, behind the stage there's laughter, there's a
din of voices coming from the bar, the record is put on,
here is Janna (Marina), 'What's your name?' 'Janna'
('Marina') smiles but doesn't look at you, she's lying on the
bedspread, ready, her arms beside her body, she nestles
herself against the curtain, with her hands above her head
she stands there, swaying her hips while you watch over
each other's shoulder her fig-leaf comes off, it falls on a
hat in the front row, you watch more intently, you jostle
in front of the vulvae which open and shut, the doors of a
cuckoo clock, older gentlemen are letting pralines burst
open between them, hold them like a rabbit's ears, others
kiss them, stick their tongue between them, the hair
tickles their faces, a quiet, heavy gentleman holds his
cigar against her, describing slow circles against the hair
which doesn't catch fire, Janna (Marina) doesn't even seem
to feel anything, sways, smiles at the cashier who is
controlling the stage lighting at the back, the record is
finished, you walk in the street the lights go on, men are
standing in a row in front of a urinal, the butchers are
letting down the iron shutters in the brightly lit frame they
walk to and fro with buckets, splashing, swabbing the
arena, the sides, the saddles are put away, the cupboard

doors slam shut, with bare forearms they scrub the blood
away while a gentleman and a lady walk in the park the
street lamps burn a thousandfold, the paths are smooth and
wide, they walk on the same ones for hours, turn into
other paths and come back to the same one, turn round,
walk in the opposite direction and come back to the same
path which is wide and smooth, bordered by lamplight and
overlooking lawns between which there are other paths
into which they turn so that they come back to the same
one, there are seats, passers-by, lovers, men with dogs,
men with their hands in their pockets, he looks at his
street plan, they are on the path which leads to the round
flowerbed which surrounds the white marble statue
representing a couple. At which point on the path are they?
Aren't they on different paths all the time? Do all the paths
look the same, so that they make it difficult to find the
way to the statue? They're walking on this path, approaching
or going further away from the statue, and discounting the
fact that they will see it, that they will presently find a way
out of this park, perhaps their walk doesn't encompass more
than three/four lawns, he points out a crossroad to her.
Does he leave the choice to her? Which of them turns
right? Which of them turns left? Does he follow her? Does
she follow him? Do they go together through the park?
Because all the paths look like each other, perhaps they
each walk on a different one, perhaps the crossroads are
pretexts to avoid the statue but also the exit, there are
two possibilities: they avoid (seek) instinctively the same,
she avoids (seeks) what he seeks (avoids). Could it be
that she feels (unconsciously) attracted to the mythological
representations which have been erected on sandstone
socles along the path, that because of these plastercasts
of masterpieces (there is moss growing in the hollows
here and there is a puddle of water) she chooses the
wrong direction? Could it be that after all he prefers to
go to the triumphal arch which looks up now and again
amongst the trees? You won't know anything about this
walk until it is completed, but not even then: perhaps you
will quite accidentally arrive at the statue just as you might
accidentally go past it you may first (without meaning to)
arrive at an exit or at the arch begins the street and the
streets where the butchers wash down the marble slabs, the

tiles sparkle in the light underneath the shutters the
water gushes on to the pavement, you walk round it,
you're wearing smart shoes, you see the group, now and
again one moves on, one joins the girls don't look at them,
they stand a little way in front of the dustbins, they're
smoking, the tallest throws her cigarette-end in front of
her on the ground, the stairs are steep, you don't touch the
handrail, the treads creak, 'Is it the first time?' 'Oh
no, no.' Did she smile at you? Did she wink? You said 'I
beg your pardon', stumbled, came towards her, very
clearly, so that she threw her cigarette-end in front of her
on the ground, stubbed it out with the toe of her shoe,
walked into the alleyway, past the dustbins Marina (Janna)
goes upstairs while you are coming downstairs the treads
creak, you come closer to the street while any moment you
expect her voice, you walk faster, you're wearing your
gloves, your glasses, the staircase resounds with her
voice, the group is bigger than it was earlier on, people
are even standing in the alleyway now, the girls are at
the bottom of the stairs, Marina (Janna) is leaning over
the banisters, you're on the stairs, not upstairs, not
downstairs, you walk past doors, up the stairs, past doors,
down the stairs, the girls come rushing up the stairs, with
brief tugs at the rail, Marina (Janna) clatters down the
stairs, policemen force their way through the alleyway.
Why did you ever get onto these stairs? Why do you want to
get away? You can avoid her/run into her on purpose, be
there at the time when she is sure to go past/cannot
possibly go past e.g. you can smile (the corners of your
mouth point slantedly upwards, your lips close a little
more tightly, curl a little, look thicker), you nod, greet
with your hand but only see her silhouette, your eye glides
past her as long as the greeting lasts it keeps moving, her
handbag is made of crocodile leather, she's got bows on
her shoes, her gaze is within your field of vision, but vague,
as is her whole face, her smile, her nod. Is she nodding?
Smiling? Looking at you? She comes round the corner, you
have just got time to cross the road, she has just got time
to start looking in a shop window, you go past in the
window, pull at your cigarette, look up at an upper storey,
look at your watch, pass through her in profile reflected in
the bunches of flowers, your head goes through the flowers

at the back, for one moment you are in the door of the
shop, you turn the corner, she can walk on, turn left at the
next crossroads, try to repeat the adventure, you watch her
from behind the net curtains, she does not glance -
apparently absentmindedly - past your window, you can
hardly interpret it as looking accidentally in your direction,
just as her glance glides - apparently accidentally - past
the front door in passing but actually past the bell-pushes
beside which the names of the tenants stand in a row above
one another, your name is somewhere in the middle, you
turn into a tree-lined road, and another one, another one
leads into a street, you turn into another street, another
one. Are you looking for her? How do you know that you
are looking for her? That you're avoiding her? Why don't
you stay in the same place all the time, i.e. in an
equilibrium of contrasts is control over yourself, over your
movements, over the vicious circle of never clear meanings,
of delusions? Is she glancing past the bell-pushes or do
you see her glancing past them? And what do you see? She's
walking past shop windows, in the windows a young woman
walks past windows, both are wearing boots with high heels,
narrow trousers, hair floating about the shoulders they
smile at each other (in each other's direction), they are
wearing a tight-fitting jacket, they admire it in the window
in which you are walking up and down through them (?), they
don't look up at all, don't notice it, go on smiling at each
other (finding each other beautiful), you sit watching closely,
the (gentle)man next to you holds his cigarette right beside
your overcoat, each row of onlookers forms a wall of backs
above which you try to see (also) her boots while she stands
with her back to the audience swaying her hips, her whip
flicks round her back, round her loins, round her thighs,
round her loins, round her back, you are all sitting in the
mirrors on either side and in the mirror in front of her
against the curtain she sways with your heads/shoulders
round her belly she flicks the whip round a neck, round a
neck, round a neck, you all swallow, crane your necks,
heads are swaying, you sweat, fumble with one hand for
your purse, with the other you hold your overcoat on your
knees, some of you their hat, you grope for a suitable
coin, some have a note ready behind their fingers, you hold
your knees apart, she's wearing a loose-fitting dress,

moves between the rows as far as possible her arm is
pale, only her face is made up, 'excuse me - excuse me -
excuse me', 'thank you - thank you - thank you -', she
doesn't look at anyone, no one looks at her either, people
look unobtrusively at her dress, at her hair which hangs
loose round her shoulders, her knees brush past your thigh
when she holds her basket at arm's length she is rather
slender are her wrists, you see little veins in the crook
of her knee, the whip lies on the stage, she picks it up,
disappears behind the curtain, you leaf through your
programme, you read the notices, change direction, keep
returning to the same street via different side-streets,
past little squares, this street must be very long,
describes (describing) an arch between others the view
often changes, you arrive in an expensive shopping street, in
a quiet neighbourhood, in a part with administrative
buildings, and still the name is the same, the numbers are
confusing, you are distracted by shop-windows, cinemas,
cafes with terraces (gentlemen, ladies are reading behind
tables, sip their coffee (they take the handle between thumb
and index finger, their little finger sticks out), flick the
ashes off their cigarette on the ash-tray it says Dortmunder,
Stout, Dubonnet, look up at you, read on i.e. look down
again, follow you (briefly) in the window, in the mirrors on
either side), you are a gentleman wearing glasses, a ring,
gloves, on the other side of the road a small crowd has
gathered, two policemen with a man emerge from an
alleyway emerges a woman, gesticulates, she wears heavy
make-up, she smokes carries a handbag, the cars brake
before the red light, you stub out your cigarette, cross the
road, join the crowd which is dispersing, some remain
behind, dawdling, the policemen slam the door of the Black
Maria, from the alleyway emerges a slim young woman
takes no notice of what is going on, walks up to the traffic
lights, crosses the road, you follow her, walking twenty
yards behind her, she turns into a side street, another one,
another one leads back to the same street, crosses it,
turns into a side street, another one, another one is
wearing boots, narrow trousers, her hair hangs down on
the collar of her close-fitting jacket, she looks at herself
in the shop windows, she arrives back in the same street,
walks past a few terraces, glances briefly at the

photographs in the hall of a cinema a man shoots from a
helicopter at a few sinister (?) fellows hiding by a lorry in
a yard a young woman looks back into the camera the bed
has not been slept in, the curtains are open. Why is she
(are you) walking through all these streets? Where does she
(do you) want to go? Why is she (are you) always coming
back to this street? What will you (will she) do when
presently she will disappear into the alleyway from which
she came, from which the handcuffed man (gentleman?)
was led by two policemen behind whom the woman with her
heavy make-up swung her handbag, gesticulated, finished
off her cigarette in four, five puffs. She throws the
cigarette end in front of her on the ground, the butchers
shuffle into the cafe, they are laughing noisily, 'Excuse
me - excuse me', a gentleman stumbles, 'Is it the first
time?' 'Oh no, no', the dustbins stand beside and on top
of each other, the men peep into the alleyway where the
other girls are smoking, indifferently, the staircase leads
past doors, past doors, past doors, the room sways on
the cable rail, she lies on the bedspread, ready, sways in
the mirrors on either side, the money is on the mantlepiece,
'I mustn't forget anything here,' you think, dustbins fall
over with a clatter, the alley is blocked, 'I want to get out
of here,' you think, the staircase is an accordion of
creaks, the stench rises from below, the men are crowding
by the door, hands in their pockets, the butcher's shops
have been scrubbed, the tiles shine, there is still a puddle on
the pavement, you walk through it on tiptoe, beams of light
fall from the empty shops, 'Look where you're going.' you
must walk more slowly, you are a gentleman, this is a
working-class neighbourhood, a shopping street.

You read i.e. you apply norms, you assert yourself in the
self-assertion of others who assert themselves in others,
others, others say 'I would', 'He would', 'They would', you
think, you walk from one room into the other, in each room
there are chairs, four round a table, one in a corner, one
by a table, one with a stocking on it, the house is full of
empty chairs, people pull them from under the table, sit
down on them, talk with their forearms resting on the
table, smoke, lean their chin in one cupped hand, stand
upright, change (exchange) chairs, drink, ask the way, walk
through other rooms, say 'We've come from elsewhere',
'We're here', 'We're going elsewhere', they greet, shake
your hand, the chairs are standing about higgledy-
piggledy, everybody smiles, you wave, the cars turn the
corner, the rooms are filled with smoke, you walk from
ashtray to ashtray, leave the glasses where they are, almost
empty, half empty/full, altogether empty, here and there
lie books, periodicals, letters, scraps of paper with
scribbles, you read, sit in a chair, in another one, you
don't move them, the fire smoulders, it's chilly, half
dark (the blinds are down, the curtains closed), you close
the front door behind you, look around the front garden,
walk along the side of the house, stand in the back garden,
walk along the other side of the house, stand in the front
garden, by the front door, uncles are sitting on chairs,
smoking, leaning backwards, laughing, nodding, aunts are
sitting in a circle, chattering, taking a(nother) biscuit,
holding their knees together, pointing significantly (?) with
their finger, a corner of the table is cleared for you, you
sit on your knees on the chair, turn the pieces of cardboard
round and round in your fingers, press them in/on to each
other, look at the shapes of the open spaces between the
cardboard on the table-top, the irregular shapes of the

cardboard, each new piece changes the shape of the
table-top, the shape of THE PUZZLE, you pull the pieces
out again, put them in another place, in another one, you
compare the pictures i.e. you try to imagine the one
before, they only differ in one, two, three pieces, 'He
still doesn't understand it', your father wants you to copy
the picture in which the boy gives a bunch of flowers to the
girl, the church spire is close by, there are cows in the
meadow, his hairy hands come near your face, pull the
bunch of flowers from under the girl's feet, take the spire
from the head of the little boy who stands there laughing
stupidly with a skirt on, the girl's stomach is made of
bricks, the cows are lying on their back in the flowers, you
clench your teeth, your father tears half the puzzle to
pieces, his elbow is just by your ear, the uncles laugh,
sip their drinks, all your work has been in vain, all
possibilities fall away, tears come to your eyes, you run
between the chairs (between the aunts), your father doesn't
come after you, your mother is probably in the kitchen, you
draw i.e. you look for proportions, on different sheets you
draw different shapes while below you you hear your father
joking, someone is rattling with plates, uncles, aunts,
mother, father look down at you, you turn your back towards
them, push the little table under your grandfather's portrait,
draw new proportions, possibilities, which you hadn't tried
out yet with the puzzle itself (which you don't want to touch
any more), you read, consult three/four books, look up
certain pages, leave a bookmark between them, you
recognize words, expressions, phrases. Have you read
this before? Here? In another place? In other places?
Is there any difference? What is it? What is the meaning?
The significance? i.e. what is it's place in the chapter? In
the book? In (the) different books? You don't understand a
word, look for its definition, of the unfamiliar words in the
definition you look up the definitions in which unfamiliar
words occur of which you look up the definition which
contains unfamiliar words of which you...Is your knowledge
increasing? Decreasing? When are you in control of
reality (?) i.e. (e.i.) the language in which you look for the
definition of an ever increasing number of words which
gradually change their meanings i.e. they occur in unfamiliar
contexts, break out of them, make the familiar (withered)

structures invalid and also the new ones, the new, the new
snow lies around the house, your footprints go from the
front door along the side of the house to the back garden,
from the back garden along the other side of the house to
the front garden, from the front garden to the front door,
from the front door to the front garden, from the front garden along the side of the house to the back garden, from
the back garden along the other side of the house to the
front door from which similar but (you can't see it, you
know) unfamiliar footprints lead along the path to the road
(onto the road, into the trampled snow), from where there
are footprints (different ones mixed up together) leading to
the front door, from the front door to the garage doors,
from the garage doors to the road, from the road to the
garage doors, from the garage doors to the front door,
you look around indecisively, you hear laughter from
within while the footprints become snowed under, smoke
rises from the two chimneys while the connection with the
road slowly disappears, people are busy arguing i.e. some
are standing in front of their chairs, one leg stretched in
front of the other one, they are wearing waistcoats, they
hook their left thumb in the armhole, drum on their chest
with the fingers of their left hand, the fingers of their
right hand are spread, resting on the table-top, 'I'm
wearing a tie', 'I smoke cigars', others lean back in their
chair, hands in their trouser pockets, beating time with
one foot, rubbing their tongue along their teeth, their
nostrils tremble, 'I'm wearing a pullover', ' I remain
seated', they also say (the ones and the others) 'Yes, maybe',
'Never completely', 'I doubt it', 'I wouldn't dare say so',
these are the answers, they sound between the statements,
together they form conversations (contacts) while you enter
and say your name, you let yourself be introduced to
everyone separately, people look at each other questioningly,
there's whispering behind your back, people laugh nervously
frown. Do they think you're pulling their leg? That you're
not quite right in the head? Is your name too common? Too
personal? Is it because everyone is so that no one is so that
you are the only one bearing everyone's name? Is it your
name? Wherein is it different from another? Is it different?
Your father shuts the box; 'Another thing we've wasted our
money on'. 'He can't do sums either', says your mother,

various people are facing the counter behind which she
stands facing a lady who puts a banknote beside the parcel
around which she ties a string, she gives the lady the
parcel, opens the drawer, takes the banknote from the
counter... Does she notice? Is she counting the notes? Can
she tell the difference between them? You took one with a
little tear, one which hadn't been folded yet, one with
stains on it, little spatters of blood from the monster that
opens his mouth while the young saint is unaware, his left
foot stands on the neck (apparently he doesn't feel anything
either, he must be blind and numb), his quiver sticks out
above his shoulders, he clutches his bow in his right hand,
listens (cocking his head) to the wind (?) which plays on
the strings, the school (the church) is in the background,
you hold the note in front of the attic window, the old man
looks suspicious, spatters from the monster in his beard,
his pupils are in the corners of his eyes, his hair is
tousled, he is jealous, your father on the stairs, too late,
he closes the attic door behind him, takes Lydia's dress
out of her hands, puts your trousers on a chair, he does
everything very slowly. Why does he look at you like that?
Is he comparing you two? Is he looking for the difference
between you? Is this the punishment? (In the Earthly
Paradise Adam and Eve were suddenly ashamed i.e. naked,
and then God came). Downstairs in the house the uncles and
aunts are talking, he won't tell them anything, forget it all,
first the two of you have to kneel down under the attic
window, your arms raised, pray an act of contrition three
times, he stands in a corner, counts your ribs, follows
your bones, the shape of your shoulder blades, he compares
the colour of your skin, your nipples, your navels, the
notes are stuck between the tiles, he picks up the drawings
from the floor, 'All those puzzles,' he says to some of his
aunts, 'The imagination of that child!', the drawings are
scattered all over the room, there are glasses standing on
them, an ashtray, no one takes any notice of them, no one
asks 'Is this yours, my boy?', 'Is this you, my boy?',
'May I have one of them?', there are smears on them,
smudges of ashes, creases, an uncle starts drawing a map,
they're all standing around him, no one suspects that this
paper is yours, he draws the road to the country house (to
the pine forest, the sandy lanes, the heath), he draws

several roads which lead to the same place, compares
them, your lines run through them like rivers, they are
crossed by bridges, you blow them up, the cars tumble in
the water, the paper is a disaster area, a cataclysm, the
culprit cannot be found, patrols are sent out, road-blocks
set up, there are interviews on television while you collect
evidence, you pin the documents side by side on the wall,
the walls of your room are covered with incriminating
evidence, undeniable facts, open confessions underneath
the photographs (the whole family looks down on them),
'They're only boys' tricks. He'll grow out of it', an uncle
says to your father who is joking once again with the aunts.
Do they understand anything? Do they see anything? Do they
ever read, you mean: do they compare lines, thickness,
length, hesitations, ways in which they avoid i.e. seek each
other, twists and turns, crossings which you follow
intently, you hold the sheet against the light, far away from
you, near your eye, you brush your hand through your hair,
walk around the room, stand still, put the paper on a chair,
sit down on your knees in front of it, turn away with a
dreamy look on your face, look again, suddenly you spring
to your feet, you stand with the paper over the waste-paper
basket, put it on the table, let the blinds down, switch the
light on, there are shadows falling on it, they form a second
drawing on top of the first one, it doesn't coincide with it, it
irritates you more than ever, the false politeness which is
intrusiveness, the uncertain lines which betray flattery,
the pretentious elegance of the middle loops, you tear the
paper, throw it into the basket, you slam the door behind you,
there are only a few footprints in the snow, one by one you
pick the snippets out of the basket, you put them side by
side, push them in their places, with sticky-tape you stick
it all together, put it away, you empty the letterbox, the
letter is exactly the same, it is simply another copy, you
thought that the first one was lost, you wrote a third, a
fourth, a fifth, that is to say, time passes (there is a
passing of time) while you compare the copies. Is there a
difference in the time of writing? Of reading? Is it only
the repetition of writing/reading? Are the words really the
same? Does one, in defiance of everything, want to
maintain the illusion that time doesn't exist, i.e. the
awareness of having read the previous letters, the proof of

the torn and glued-together copies which have been tidied
away, their presence makes self-delusion more and more
difficult (ridiculous), their number grows while the words
don't change, the margin remains the same width, the ink
remains the same but fades, this is it: the sheets grow
yellow in the folder, the tears differ from sheet to sheet, you
copy the letters, multiply the copies, cut out individual
letters, syllables, words, clauses, sentences are lying in
a jumble on the attic floor, you construct syllables, words,
clauses, sentences, paragraphs, letters which are
differenc and contain the same words, they have the same
appearance, the situation becomes more and more
complicated, the sheets are overcrowded, you cross out
words, you write above, underneath, beside them, writing
and crossing out keep each other in equilibrium, the text
becomes unclear, blurred, the sheet is white like snow,
teems with meanings, is utterly illegible, i.e. the
legibility (visibility) is unlimited while around you people
are writing, that is to say, are limiting, restricting
legibility, they write on beer-spills, on sheets of writing
paper, on programmes, in exercise books, leave them
casually on the tablo, thcy are left lyliig about, put away
somewhere so that you've got to start looking for them,
you read through them, suspicions, guesses, expectations,
disillusions arise, 'We've met before', I think. Aren't you
the man who'... someone asks, 'Is this your real name or',
(as if the name which you present to him on a card would
be different from the one by which you want to be known,
with which you join in the game, your personal stake, the
risk you consider the safest, - and this changes according
to circumstances, to the years, to the company you're in),
'You've changed', (they mean: 'You're no longer the same'),
while they look at you they distantiate themoolvco from you
(take their distance from you, keep themselves at a
distance) that's to say they see (feel) how you distantiate
yourself i.e. you see (through) what they do, they don't let
themselves be caught (humiliated), formal exuberance
becomes formal reservation, they join in the game, you
lead it but (it leads) to nothing, two gentlemen are
exuberant, cool, serious, ironic... What does it matter?
What difference is there between the puzzles of the moment
at which they are put together harmoniously, the cardboard

pieces fit into each other, each cardboard piece fits in
the whole (does not look out of place) that is to say the
relations between the pieces vary and remain the same.
Is there a relation between the pieces or between the
places where they belong, their colours, their shapes,
their design? Are the pieces (also) something other than
their place, their colour, shape, design? You stand in a
corner of the room, you sniff at a plush easy chair in
which a slim lady was sitting before, at the spilt ashes on
(your) paper, ('Say: hellow auntie, hello uncle'. 'Hello, my
boy', they stroke you hair. 'He's a sturdy looking lad, ' they
say to your father, to your mother, they don't say your
name (Do they know it?), they don't ask it, 'You go and
play again', says your father), you try to reconstruct the
situations, the place where that fat one slapped with his
hand on the table, roaring with laughter (a red face, knees
wide apart, his short fat arms gesticulating while someone
knocks the ashes from his cigarette, leans back, asks a
question), the lady in the plush chair (What colour was her
dress? Was she wearing any bracelets? She was smoking,
yes: she moved the tip of her tongue along her lips, one
hand was beside her head, the other on her knee.) got up,
took her handbag, walked through the lobby, through the
bedroom. (Here she looked out of the window. She saw
Japanese cherry trees, dustbins still standing at the
roadside, with boxes beside them, tins, peelings, old
newspapers lie in the snow, cars rush by this way and that,
streetlamps are burning.) Did she find the switch? Did she
leave the bedroom door open? So that she could see by the
light from the window, from the streetlamps, while two
gentlemen were talking in a whisper, sometimes the one
raised his hand to his mouth, said something into the
other one's ear, they snort with laughter, the other one
made an ambiguous (deterrent) joke to two ladies who were
clearly looking for an opportunity to contribute their little
aside, the conversation in the group had more or less
fallen silent, suddenly the two gentlemen were very
conspicuously standing apart in the corner by the door, the
fat one fell silent, the lady came back into the room with
her handbag, the smoke was floating towards the ceiling,
glasses, drinks, cups were standing about all over the
place, a cigarette was smouldering in an ashtray, someone

switched on the radio while the lady sat down again, she
put one leg over the other, smoothed down her skirt,
laughed (nervously), the conversation was resumed
hesitantly i.e. the presence of the two in the corner faded
(people didn't want to show their curiosity, their envy),
someone looked at his watch, others could now look as well,
express their surprise at the passing of time, of the hours
which are passed in (pleasant) conversation, just once more
the fire was raked up, one more log (it alleviates the pain,
it's a rule of the game) was put on it, people started making
ready to go (the scene became more lively, everyone smiled,
looked animated, people were tapping on each other's shoulders), you stand with your hands in your pockets, looking at
the tracks, the road is deserted, you put your overcoat on,
drive your car out of the garage, shut the doors, the
house is now altogether alone, you drive away (from it),
past streetlights, villas, shops, blocks of flats, you draw
tracks through in tracks, it has stopped snowing, streets,
crossroads, traffic lights, bends, look like/look
different from each other. Where are the guests? The
voices, glances, gestures, the hubbub, the laughter? The
house stands in the lamplight, the blinds are down, the rooms
are full of smoke, you smell the beer, pull the cover over
your head, curl up, pull your legs up, your nightshirt right
over your feet, you're completely inside it, you carefully
caress your nipples with your knees, you stick your face
through the neck of your nightshirt, stroke your chest with
your chin, with your finger you stroke your willie, you
keep your eyes closed, the door opens, the light shines
fiercely, the bedcovers are turned back, they pull at you,
hit you, can't get your knees apart, your fingers are
riveted together round your legs, your teeth are clenched,
they can tear your nightshirt off, kick you out of bed, call,
shout, open the curtains, the windows (they won't, surely!!),
'You naughty boy', say the aunts, you stick out your tongue
at them, run away between them, your grandfather is already
waiting in the snow, you leave the house behind you, that of
the neighbours, the third, the fourth, you turn the corner,
your grandfather doesn't like the aunts, your father, he
gives you a spade, in the vegetable garden you dig a round
hole (it has no corners), you put branches over it, foliage,
walk (apparently casually) through the garden, step on it,

you close the hole above you, the sunlight forms a jigsaw
puzzle on the bottom, on you, you turn round, forever
different specks fall on different places you press your
head between your knees while your back is teeming with
specks of light you have underneath you an untouched spot,
you look at it intently, slowly you close your eyes: 'What
do you think of it?', 'I suppose you noticed?', 'I mean, I
assume you noticed the difference?', 'In any case you will
have compared it with?', 'Don't you agree that these
similarities are obvious?'. 'Do you think there's anything
new in it?'. You smile, answer evasively, shake hands
with them (take leave), while the cars turn in the road you
wave, they drive slowly to the corner, you go back indoors
you choose a chair, one on the outer side, you sit with
your hand under your chin. You look around the room.

A buzzing swells (approaches), fades, changes into a
buzzing which swells fades, changes into a swelling
buzzing (a movement) of which you try to guess the
direction, you sit with your face turned to the wall, the
traffic is equally busy in both directions, often there is at
the same moment, and hardly distinguishable from each
other, a swelling and a fading, cars pass each other in
front of the house, dull rumblings and screeches can be
heard simultaneously, you can recognize certain makes,
ways of pulling up, braking, handling gears, you imagine
how they catch up as they pass the avenue, cars are
waiting to turn into the main road, they pull up, change
gears, the droning fades away. When the blinds at the front
have not been lowered, you can watch them: one after the
other they rise above the hump of the bridge, descend,
sweep past the avenue, past the front gardens, climb,
disappear behind the bridge, brake, wait with flashing
lights till a line of oncoming cars has gone past, pull up,
with a heavy drone they turn into the avenue, past the front
gardens, between the trees, the villas, the wide footpaths
on which the neighbours' children play ball, hopscotch, skip,
several cars are parked in the drives. While you read you
follow intently the coming and going of the sounds, you look
at your watch, a light car approaches, the driver brakes
noisily (forcefully), waits (flashes), turns into the avenue,
slows down, you wait for the heavy drone (the slow (careful)
driving onto the kerb), the honk, you spring up, run
through the rooms, rush down the steps, in the dark you walk
through the garage, grope for the door handle, push the doors
open, the road is deserted, A CAR goes by, waits at the
corner, slowly turns into the main road, is overtaken, an
oncomer flashes, one by one cars emerge from behind the
corner house, speed past the avenue, climb, disappear,

rise above the hump of the bridge, descend, let an
oncoming car pass which is waiting with flashing lights,
turns into the avenue, in front of the house he changes
gear, one of the children opposite is standing in the door,
you close the doors, the droning, rushing, buzzing continues,
you look at your watch, a car turns into the avenue, slows
down, drives onto the gravel, a door slams shut while you
are clutching the door handle, a car drives up to the main
road, underneath you a goods train emerges from the
viaduct, the car descends while another one rises on the
viaduct, descends, followed by another one while the driver
frequently looks in the mirror in which you are watching
him, your auntie Milly smiles at you, her face is in the
mirror, then it looks serious again like that of the driver
which moves to and fro beside and in front of hers (hers
moves beside and behind that of the driver), oncoming
traffic rushes past (you rush past oncoming traffic), crossroads, villages, a river, you encounter cyclists, you sit
hand in hand in the back seat, the sun plays on your faces,
the driver smokes, looks in the mirror in which your
auntie Milly keeps looking rigidly ahead, the driver flashes
his lights, turns into the drive which curves in a crescent
to the steps, you climb them, your auntie Milly's heels
tap on the shiny tiles, she walks down the corridors, hesitates at a side-passage, reads the numbers, she takes the
lift, on another (?) floor you walk through the same (?)
corridors, walk down the stairs, read the numbers, all the
doors are the same, the distance between them is the same
everywhere, there are little lights above them. Where is
your grandfather? Is he behind one of these doors which is
the same as and different from all the others? Isn't it all
the same on which door your aunty Millie knocks? Isn't
your grandfather a thousand times present here? Does it
give your auntie Milly a fright when a door opens? You look
into a room, through the window you see the park, the sun
falls on the bed, 'Hello grandfather', but it isn't him, he
gets up, he's wearing his tailcoat, he is grumpy, you can't
hear what he says, the monstrance from the high altar
stands on the mantlepiece, your auntie Milly pushes you
back into the corridor, maybe your grandfather isn't here
at all. Can he be here? Whatever made your auntie Milly
look for him here? How can you find your grandfather

behind hundreds of doors which are the same i. e. the
windows are the same, the beds, the rooms, the grand-
fathers? Where is he then? You stick the flower under your
vest, the thorns tickle (titillate), 'Undress me', you say,
you lie on your back, Lydia rubs your chest with the flower,
she strews the petals all over you, she rolls the stem up
and down under her hand, you groan, she licks the spots of
blood, undresses, a warm and supple body lies on top of
yours, you have drunk wine, you are very tired, above you
the water moves. Is it moving? You look about you, you run
to the top of the dune, trudge down through the sand, arrive
panting on the top of another dune, call, she is lying somewhere in the sand, laughing. At the same place as earlier
on? At a different place? Which was the place of earlier on?
Which earlier on? Your grandfather walks at the same
times in the same places, he notes every change, going
along the tree-lined walk around the town he is unchangeable,
a clockhand which by means of absolute precision keeps
points of time and points of place in equilibrium and
through movement (apparently) maintains immobility. He
lights the lamps, his silhouette moves, he has a right arm,
cuffs, a goatee, a left arm, a jacket, two arms with hands
with fingers between which smoke rises to above the screen
which is stretched between you and him, behind which he is
vaguer <u>and</u> clearer, black and sharply outlined, he lowers
the pup<u>pet</u>s, fades away, you only <u>hear</u> him now, and you
hear <u>him</u>, more distinct than if you <u>saw</u> him at the same
time <u>are</u> these sounds of the old man with the walking stick
who combs your hair with a parting in the middle, who asks
(he bends over to you, puts his hand on your shoulder, a
palm, a thumb, fingers): Do you like this? What do you like
best? The music makes the puppets move (the puppets set
the music in motion), the princess walks (flees) round and
round, while the treacherous courtier walks behind her (is
after her). Is the princess walking in front of the courtier?
Is the courtier walking in front of the princess? The
courtier gains ground (the princess loses), the courtier loses
ground (the princess gains) and these are the princess and
the treacherous courtier: you recognize their splendid
clothes, the gold, the scarlet, the lace, the embroidery, the
pink skin, the frightened, innocent look, the dark, furrowed
face, the covetous look, you recognize the colours from the

movements, the eyes from the arms, the music i.e. the
suspense i.e. the speed mounts till in the middle of the
screen a sword breaks the pursuit, three figures stand
motionlessly in the silence in which a soft buzz (a slight
movement, a gesture) becomes audible (visible), the
crossing of daggers, the positioning of the opponents
slowly and languidly introduces the duel which starts off
with a sudden thrust, a blow, with straight (proud) and
bent (spying) postures, the dance accelerates, in the top
right hand corner the princess hides her face in her hands,
on the left, below, there is a turning wheel of legs,
daggers, arms, bodies, heads. Who is winning? Who has
been hit? Are they hitting each other? When? Whereabouts?
The daggers connect the two figures, are part of them,
make them into a figure which is battling (moving) against
himself, that's to say this figure sees himself, reacts to
the image it has of itself. What is this figure? What is its
(reflected) image? What is their relation with the princess
(what have they got to do with her)? What is the relationship
between the princess and each of them, i.e. what will
happen when the outcome has become clear, the shorter,
broader figure (the treacherous one) tumbles into the void,
the slimmer one turns towards the princess who is
screaming (during the fight her screams sounded as if they
came from between the daggers, from between the two men),
she stands with her hands before her face, turning away
(turning towards), the knight raises his hand (calls out a
greeeting), your grandfather appears on the screen again,
he lets the puppets sink away, he coughs, shuffles,
clatters about, coughs, smoke rises behind the net curtains,
neighbours walk past, a motorist brakes, flashes (?),
turns into the avenue, slows down, you are ready, the
wheels scrunch on the gravel, you run through the rooms,
hurry down the steps, walk through the garage, grope for
the handle, let the doors turn back. Are you really expecting
anyone? Anyone in particular? Are you dreading his/her
arrival? Are you looking forward to it? Are you looking
forward to dreading that a (the) car will stop in the drive,
you wave, you beckon that the garage is free (you invite),
the car descends, moves beside you, stops in front of the
old tyres which stand against the wall, serving as bumpers
in clumsy (rough) manoeuvres, you open the door, smile,

greet i.e. talk and make a bow, let the other pass first,
take the other's coat, lead into the house, pull up the
blinds, open the net curtains, neighbours walk in their
garden, glance (accidentally) through the window, you are
engaged in lively conversation, you pour out, smoke,
stand with one hand in your pocket, smile, sit down. Are
you pleased? Have you been waiting for this all the time?
The neighbours smile, they think this is a very pleasant
villa with a distinguished, pleasant owner, a gentleman who
receives a visit from someone who arrives in a very
expensive car, who talks, drinks, smiles, sits in easy
chairs, stands up and puts one hand in his trouser pocket,
the door to the terrace is open, he calmly walks into the
garden with the visitor, smiling, joking, pointing out
plants, he looks into the house where there are easy chairs,
a glass-top coffee table, lamps, ashtrays, glasses with
drinks, there are authentic paintings on the walls, the
fitted carpet, bookshelves, a briefcase on a chair, it is
all clearly and as if reflected behind the windows in which
you walk past with a distinguished gentleman/an elegant
lady who is taking (an interested?) part in the conversation
while the cars roar past on the main road (you hardly hear
them), 'Good morning, good morning', you say to the
neighbours, cheerfully, very amiably, they return the
greeting, 'The weather isn't too bad, is it', they agree,
greet again, he holds the car door open, she gets in, slowly,
amiably, gracefully they drive to the corner, turn into the
main road, on the table in front of you there is a sheet of
paper with six figures on it, large and one underneath the
other, two are the same, after the 6 you write a 9, after the
5 a 3, you hesitate. Is it a 6 or a 9? A 5 or a 3? Which is
the correct order? You make combinations, try to imagine
the white paper with the correct figures above, after each
other, you fill the paper up, cross out (select), add new
numbers, you walk around the room, one by one you copy
them on sheets of white paper, one number per sheet, the
figures two by two, you put the papers on the cupboard, on
the table, the carpet, the chairs, you shut your eyes, open
them suddenly, look at one of the papers, force yourself to
remember, to recognize, you look more intently (as if you
can't read the figures), hold the paper in your hand, turn it
round, shut your eyes, open them suddenly, go to a sheet

of paper, look at it against the light, from very close by,
from further away, you turn it round, shut your eyes, you
have a few sheets (numbers) left. Are you hoping that the
right one (correct one) is among them? Are you hoping for
an error? You dial a number, with thumping heart you hear
the telephone ringing in a house/a flat/an office, in your
own neighbourhood/in another town, a man/woman reaches
for the receiver, you clear your throat, take a deep breath,
apologize, hang up, dial a number, listen, the ringing
goes on for a long time, the telephone rings in a room with
closed shutters, in a house with an empty garage, they have
gone out, you don't put the receiver back, you can dial this
number for hours on end, let the telephone ring ten, twenty
times, you become more reckless, listen only half as it
rings, dial again, it goes on ringing, you dial again, it
goes on ringing. Is this the right number? What was it you
were going to say? Some time, when the receiver is picked
up (this will inevitably happen, it is, after all, desirable)
you will have to have your words ready, all the time you
must have your opening sentence in your mind, you must be
calm in order to hear (understand) what the other person
says (means), in order to weigh your words, to maintain a
balance between appealing and repelling, you must dare
listen, look, act, not run away but push a pillow under his
head, the house is empty, the sun shines through the net
curtains on the dark red carpet which is crowded with
patterns, thin little snakes coil round your grandfather who
is lying in the middle of a pond breathing heavily, his hands
and his face are covered with tiny hairs, with streaks of
shadow, of sun, he looks very red, he's going to suffocate,
he's been poisoned, he's turning terrifyingly limp, his
head droops onto one shoulder, the hands fall open, he is
part of the carpet, when he is carried away the patterns
become meaningless, the carpet becomes a frame from
which the painting has been removed, a framed piece of
floor, of hundreds, thousands of footsteps which are no
longer there, they were there (existed) only for a moment
(Did they exist? In what way?), glasses are raised,
people laugh, talk, stand with one hand in a pocket, footsteps cross one another on the carpet, make tracks, run in
opposite/in the same directions, are everywhere and
nowhere, your grandfather is lying like a log in the middle

of an inextricable (inscrutable) labyrinth of directions.
Are the patterns moving? Are they immobile? Is only the
eye moving? The sun, which gradually changes the shadows
cast by the little hairs, the direction of the shadows, their
length? How long can this last: you in this empty house,
looking at the carpet with your grandfather, flushed,
panting, immobile? Footsteps crunch on the gravel, on the
path, the key is stuck in the front door, the sun dives,
your grandfather is sweating, the front door is closed,
the (?) footsteps tap on the floor of the lobby, on the stairs,
you are not taking your eyes from the door which remains
closed, someone is standing behind it (Is anyone standing
behind it?), footsteps crunch on the gravel, on the path,
the key is stuck in the front door, the sun dives, your
grandfather sweats, the front door slams shut, footsteps
tap in the lobby, on the stairs, you take a step back to the
window, you climb on the roof of the kitchen, Mr. and Mrs.
Candlemaker can see you, 'The little boy is on the roof of
the kitchen,' they say (they accuse, they provoke), you
can't jump into the garden: then they'll be able to see you
from the house (Is there anyone in the house? Is there no
one?), you're wearing your linen shorts, brown socks,
sandals, a cotton T-shirt, your arms are brown, your lips
chapped, you keep your eye on the windows at the back of
the houses, you can't distinguish anything behind the net
curtains from where the whole neighbourhood can watch you,
you can't go back inside. Why not? Why yes? The trees in
the garden sway, in the windows darker shadows are
swaying, gigantic swarms of bees are moving in front of
the net curtains behind which your grandfather lies. Is he
still lying there? Would you have been able to help him?
How? The leaves haven't got a particular shape (are not
identical), they are curled, facing all directions, there
is a teeming of shadows, you're standing in the midst of
the swarms of bees, your face is full of holes which are
squirming, you take a step backward, turn right (to the
edge of the roof), to the left (to the other edge), you move
very close to the window, you are being eaten by thousands
of bees, you close your eyes, the sun plays on your skin,
the boys have blindfolded you, they've pulled your trousers
down, tied your hands, they bump into you, 'Excuse me',
they say, 'I beg your pardon', 'I didn't mean to', you call

out, you cry, you spit, they roar with laughter. Are there
any girls watching? Giggling behind a fence? Feeling
sorry? Two girls are coming from another direction, you
keep your hand in your grandfather's hand, the girls giggle,
they look at you, at your grandfather, they whisper something in each other's ear, they know you, know it, laugh at
you, the walk has just been raked, you are alone with the
two girls and your grandfather who must not notice anything.
Does he feel how your hand is getting clammy? Can he feel
your blood beating in your wrist? Is he looking at you? You
walk on stiffly, the girls are approaching, they aren't
allowed to come here by themselves. Or are they? 'You
must never look at them', says your grandfather. 'They are
common children, they're shameless'. The girls brush past
you, you smell their hair, their dresses, the wide strips of
grass on either side have been mown, here and there lie a
branch, a few leaves, just as if you'd put them there
unobtrusively but nicely arranged, but your grandfather
isn't looking at them, he's looking crossly in front of him,
he has felt your hand, the thumping, he has looked at your
face, the walk is straight, the seats on either side are
empty, there is no wind, you arrive at the main road, your
grandfather looks left and right (at you), crosses the road
with your hand compellingly in his, you're on the next walk
which is straight and long, it has (just) been tidied, the
grass has been mown, there is no wind, the seats are all
empty, will the two girls come from the other direction?
Mr. and Mrs. Candlemaker? You come to the road, cross
it with your grandfather, you're on the next walk, your
feeling of shame at your feeling of shame isn't going away,
your grandfather doesn't say a word, you can feel from his
hand that he feels what you think, he compels you to go on
feeling ashamed, right beside him, moving from one walk
to the next, the water flows slowly between the shrubs,
birds chirp, the walks form a circle round the town, they
never end, they begin there where the two girls come
towards you from the opposite direction, they giggle,
whisper something in each other's ear, they know. What
does your grandfather know? He moves the princess.
Without him you would be alone with her, the prince and the
courtier have disappeared, you are facing each other while
your grandfather pulls the strings, she has 2, 6, 10, 4, 8

arms. Is he moving different princesses which are
hanging one behind the other? Are the arms casting shadows
which are casting shadows which in their turn are making
shadows gliding in and out of one another? Which are the
arms? Which the shadows? Does she actually exist? Is she
only shadows with which your grandfather keeps you under
a spell, he makes her dance very fast so that you can't
distinguish her real shape for a moment. Which is her real
shape? Does she only consist of movements i.e. of the
movements which your grandfather is making behind (in
front of) the screen while you are crouched in front of
(behind) the same screen while the princess is hanging like
a lobster, like an oriental goddess (like someone hanged?),
dancing, perhaps she will embrace you, shadows are all
around you in the room, they form a network, the screen
wrinkles, you swim in the middle of a pond in which the
shadows of the trees are swaying, the water makes them
sway, you make the water sway, the movement of water and
shadow is only a consequence of your movements, there is
no one near you, you are racing round the water with Sniff,
you roll in the grass with him amongst the bushes, you run
after him, he runs from one path to the next, arrives at
the pond, disappears behind the shrubs, you are panting,
sweating. Could there be any girls here? A man, a woman,
peeping behind a tree, watching a naked boy running after
a dog? Mr. and Mrs. Kaersmakers? Sniff runs across a
country lane, in the distance a cyclist approaches, you're
in a different (part of the) wood. Only because you saw the
country lane, the man on the bicycle, do you know that
you're in a different part, you can't call Sniff back, he
runs through a corn-field, in front of you to the right
there is a red roof with a dormer window. Where is he?
Where is the pond? You hear someone panting close by, a
big boy is lying on top of a girl, he's moving up and down,
she groans, she stretches her arms behind her head.
Where are your clothes? Cars are roaring past behind the
corn, they cross each other, pull up, someone sounds the
horn. Is Sniff crossing the road? How long can this go on:
the sun, the corn, the boy who is kissing the girl, he
suddenly half raises himself, lies down higher up, she
closes her legs, pulls up her knees between his. Is your
auntie Milly driving past in a taxi? Has she found your

clothes? Do your father, your mother, your grandfather
think you've got drowned? Across the water the chimney of
the brewery sticks out above the trees, horses whinny,
there is no wind, gardeners from the council are mowing
the strips of grass, raking, looking round at a boy who is
walking shyly and with red eyes in the middle of the path,
women are beating carpets, chat with each other from their
windows, the backs of the houses are full of windows with
net-curtains. The walk is empty, you look as far as you
can, where all the lines come together in a point which
remains always at the same distance and comes nearer at
each step (step by step), which comes into existence at
each step and becomes a stretch of path, that is to say at
each step your grandfather emerges from it, Mr. and Mrs.
Candlemaker. You make an about turn, the straight lines
of the path join at a point (Is it the same one? Wherein does
a point differ from a point? Does it exist?) which comes
nearer at each step, comes into existence and becomes a
stretch of path that is to say your grandfather emerges from
it, Mr. and Mrs. Candlemaker. You escape into a side
lane which descends steeply to the water. There is no one
there. Here and there among the grass on the verge, the
nettles, the bushes, the torn newspapers, there lies a turd.
Frogs are jumping about. On the walk, which is closed off
by shrubs and trees, people are passing by. You hear a
man's voice, a woman's voice. The water has light and dark
patches, children (?) have thrown stones into it, weeping
willows are hanging over it like curtains. Is your grandfather coming down the walk? Wearing his tail-coat? His
bowler hat? Is he leaning on his walking stick, listening to
the birds which are singing in the trees between you? On
the main road a buzzing swells (comes closer), fades
away, changes into a buzzing which swells, fades away,
changes into a swelling buzzing (a movement) of which you
try to guess the direction, you get up, turn round. The
neighbours are walking in the garden, smiling.

the ship is beside the house waves the water reflects the ship
sails that is to say the houses glide past glides the ship
along a line consists of points move away i.e. come nearer
despair is hope is despair is interpretation is standing with
your face towards the houses stand with their faces towards
the water connects them with houses are between this sailing
is neither backwards not forwards whistles the steam in a
circle is the wind in the direction of the moment changes
from south to west to north to east are efforts which cancel
each other out while the ship sails from the harbour which
you see to the harbour which you don't see is the harbour
which you see the blue ship in the blue water makes a blue
ship makes blue water makes a shore makes a shore makes
a distance between which blue water is between two shores
are connected by a ship makes houses have streets have
towers have views loom up that is to say fade away in
sailing on the water carries the ship is on the way that is
to say is ship is only ship when it is on the way that is in the
(distant) view of houses are only houses when they stay in
one place i.e. in the (distant) view of the water makes the
ship makes the shores where the best sailors stay either
standing on the ship or standing on the shore is longing for
standing on the ship is longing for the shore is a vicious
circle within which the water goes up and down under the
ship the land moves further from shore to shore does not
exist except in longing for water i.e. moving away i.e.
moving towards only lasts as long as a shore is in sight
sails a ship without a shore is a house without water waves
innumerable are the waves are unrecognizably identical
going up and down is uncertain(ty) is lack of direction is
forwards or backwards is no different is wel(l)fare is
saying fare-well to sea-faring the blind do not see the
water just as the deaf do not hear the wind which whistles

in a circle sails the ship in a circle stand the houses see
no ship sees no houses are purposeless is purposeless is
land surrounds water surrounds land is everywhere a
begetter of water is everywhere a begetter of land and why
does the one call the other calls the one steadily they beget
discord leads from the one to the other to the one will see
the blind will hear the deaf will see one one one and the same
is two is the image of the one is the image of the other is
longing wistfulness envy discord arises from seeing is a
consequence of hearing is suspecting by the man suspects
the woman suspects the woman suspects the man suspects
the man sails forth i. e. takes leave of himself seeks
himself in a circle sailing within himself is the water is
outside him is the water is until the land is invisible A
CIRCLE around the water carries the ship loses its goal
is the shore is out of sight comes longing wistfulness envy
discord between the house and the ship sails alone stands
the house in a house and a ship in a ship you sailed a mirror
is water does not exist the union of longing and longed for
is an effort is a cause of everything (is the ship is the house
is the water is the land) is a desert is the wind is a whistle
is a circle passes from east to south to west to north over
the water makes the ship ever smaller i. e. larger i. e.
smaller circles within the circle of the shore in the circle
of the houses is reflected in the water reflects the ship
comes nearer i. e. moves further away despair is hope is
despair is a (stand)point is a (view)point is an interpretation
a way out is a mirror is the house a mirror is the land a
mirror is the water recedes from the land disappears the
house i. e. the ship disappears.

SIGNATURE is a new series of shorter works, distinguished by the highly personal and imaginative approach
of the author to his subject. It comprises works of poetry
and prose, fiction and non-fiction, and includes English,
American, and translated texts.

Signature 1
DARKER ENDS by Robert Nye poems

Signature 2
OLT by Kenneth Gangemi novel

Signature 3
THE CARNAL MYTH by Edward Dahlberg
     essay

Signature 4
THE THEATRE AND ITS DOUBLE
     by Antonin Artaud essays

Signature 5
SHARDS by Nick Rawson prose poem

Signature 6
ENEMIES by Reinhard Lettau sketches

Signature 7
REFLECTIONS by Mark Insingel novel

Signature 8
A BLACK MANIFESTO IN
JAZZ POETRY AND PROSE
     by Ted Joans

Signature 9
LESSNESS by Samuel Beckett prose

Signature 10
STORIES FOR CHILDREN by Peter Bichsel
     short stories

Signature 11
IMAGES OF AFRICA by Aidan Higgins
    <u>diaries</u>

Signature 12
PRISON POEMS by Yuli Daniel <u>poems</u>

Signature 13
POLITICS AND LITERATURE by Jean-Paul Sartre
    <u>essays and interviews</u>